Amigas

Playing for Keeps

Amigas
Playing for Keeps

by Veronica Chambers

Created by Jane Startz
Inspired by Jennifer Lopez

Hyperion
New York

Copyright © 2011 Jane Startz Productions and Nuyorican Productions

SXSW® and South by Southwest® are registered trademarks of SXSW Inc.

All rights reserved. Published by Hyperion, an imprint of Disney Book Group. No part of this book may be reproduced or transmitted in any form or by any means, electronic or mechanical, including photocopying, recording, or by any information storage and retrieval system, without written permission from the publisher. For information address Hyperion, 114 Fifth Avenue, New York, New York 10011-5690.

Printed in the United States of America
First Edition
1 3 5 7 9 10 8 6 4 2

J689-1817-1-11001

Library of Congress Cataloging-in-Publication Data on file

ISBN 978-1-4231-2365-1

Designed by Jennifer Jackman

Visit www.hyperionteens.com

For Magda and Sophia, mis sobrinas queridas.
—*V.C.*

For all my amigas—*Adin, Ellen, Helen, Robin, Kate, Zoë, Marika, Wendy, Marie, Judy, Jen, Cheryl, and Mazal. Thanks for enriching my life. And for Peter and Jesse—you've both got game.*
—*J.S.*

CHAPTER 1

FIFTEEN-YEAR-OLD Alicia Cruz did not start her *quinceañera* planning business to be popular. As the wealthy and beautiful daughter of one of Miami's most prominent power couples, she'd never lacked for friends. But ever since Alicia, along with her best friends—Carmen Ramirez-Ruben, Jamie Sosa, and Gaz Colón (who was now Alicia's boyfriend as well)— had formed Amigas Incorporated and in the process planned more than twenty of the hottest Sweet Fifteen parties in the greater Miami area, her profile at Coral Gables High School had never been higher.

Every afternoon, when the four friends sat at their table in the school cafeteria—second from the right, near the sliding doors, with floor-to-ceiling views of the school's lush, tropical campus—they were flooded with visits from C. G. High students hoping to get a little free *quince* advice.

On this particular Thursday, Alicia, Carmen, and Jamie had just sat down to eat a lunch supplied by Maribelle Puentes, the Cruz family cook and Alicia's de facto grandmother. Maribelle had recently started dating Tomás, a Peruvian Japanese chef from the trendy restaurant Nobu Miami, and as a testament to their relationship had added sushi-making to her repertoire of already impressive culinary skills.

Alicia handed both of her friends a small tin *bento* box, professionally packed in an insulated bag.

"Maribelle wanted you guys to try some, too," Alicia explained, opening her lunchbox to reveal twelve perfect, restaurant-quality Japanese sushi rolls. "I'm in heaven," she sighed. "Yellowtail scallion rolls."

"Spicy shrimp tempura hand rolls, my favorite," Jamie said, tucking in to her sushi.

Carmen, who'd already popped a bite of tuna tataki into her mouth, pointed to her face and offered a thumbs-up. "*Chicas*," she sighed contentedly when she finished chewing, "I truly don't think our lives could get any better than this—sunny weather, yummy food, and hot boyfriends. How cool is that?"

She wasn't lying. Her hot boyfriend was Domingo Quintero, a senior at Hialeah High and a waiter at Bongos, the group's favorite restaurant, which was famous for its frequent celebrity sightings and delicious virgin *mojitos*. Not only was he super good-looking, he also happened to be supernice.

Earlier that year, Jamie had started dating Dash Mortimer, a golf star who was also heir to a considerable fortune. Dash was not your typical Latin guy, which had caused some issues when he first showed interest in hotheaded Jamie. His late mom had been a Venezuelan beauty queen, and his father traced his family's lineage back to the *Mayflower*. Amigas Inc. had been hired to plan a *quince* for Binky, Dash's socialite sister, which was how he had met Jamie. They both fell hard. A fierce salsa dancer, Dash moved with the confidence of a gifted athlete, and had been the only guy to break down the tough-girl exterior Jamie had rocked since she'd moved to Miami from the Bronx.

"Speaking of boyfriends, I wish Gaz was here," Alicia said with a sigh.

Alicia and Gaz—an aspiring musician, a founding member of Amigas Inc., and formerly one of Alicia's best friends—had been officially dating now for about a year. "You know how obsessed he is with sushi," she added, "not to mention Maribelle's cooking. My bet is that he's still in the music room, working on some new songs."

Unfortunately, talk about boyfriends was going to have to be put on hold, because it appeared someone needed their help. The someone was a classmate of theirs, a boy named Nesto.

"Sorry to interrupt," he said, coming to stand at the head of their table. "I just have a quick question. This girl I really like, Tia, asked me to be her *chambelán de honor* at her *quinceañera*."

"That sounds great," Jamie said, causing both Alicia and Carmen to smile. Since Jamie had started dating Dash, she had become more comfortable showing her softer side—a welcome change for her two best friends, who in the past had often found themselves apologizing to their clients for their friend's extreme bluntness and occasionally acid tongue.

"Congrats," Carmen mumbled, since he'd caught her in midchew.

"Thanks. I can't wait," he said. "It's not an Amigas Inc. joint, but it should be a good party all the same."

"So, how can we help?" Alicia asked, getting right to the point.

"I really like this girl," Nesto said. "But I've got about fifty dollars to get her a *quince* present. All my boys say you've got to drop at least a C-note for something nice."

"Not true," Jamie said.

"Not at all," Alicia agreed, finishing up her last piece of sushi.

"Well, I went to the Gap. . . ." Nesto said.

"Not the Gap!" cried Carmen.

"Why not?" asked Nesto, looking perplexed.

"Never the Gap for a *quince*!" Jamie piped up. "That's where you go to buy your back-to-school clothes, not the special something for the girl of your dreams. You know what *would* be perfect?"

Nesto shrugged. "I don't. That's why I came to you guys."

"A charm bracelet," Alicia said.

"Silver," Carmen added.

Jamie took out a card and said, "Go to Key and Ree. Ask for Josefina. She'll help you pick out something nice."

"And there's a ten percent discount for Amigas Inc. clients," Alicia added. "Tell her we sent you."

Nesto was all smiles as he glanced down at the card and then back at them. "You guys are the best."

"Glad we could help," Alicia said.

But there was no rest for the weary. As soon as Nesto walked away, a girl named Liya ran up to their table.

"Hey, I know I'm not one of your clients, but I could really use some advice," she said.

Alicia looked at her watch. "We've got a few more minutes. What's up?"

"I'm having a Nancy Drew *quince*," Liya said.

The girls exchanged curious and amused glances.

"Yeah, I'm really excited. We're doing a whole murder-mystery game thing. And I need to figure out some favors for one hundred people. And needless to say, I'm on a budget, or I would have totally hired you guys."

"Hmm, a Nancy Drew–themed favor," Alicia said. "That's a tough one."

She took out her phone and started searching for some options. Thirty seconds later, she had an answer.

"This Web site has a free Nancy Drew bookmark you can download," Alicia said.

"Then go and get them printed and laminated," Jamie added.

"Don't forget to put a picture of you in your *quince* dress on the back," Carmen suggested.

"If you have the loot, you could punch a hole in the top and tie a ribbon and add a little chain with your initials," Jamie said.

Once the *amigas* started giving *quince* advice, even pro bono, it was hard for them to stop.

"Perfect!" Liya said, her eyes lighting up. "I'll order

them tonight. I would never have thought of this. You rock!"

"We aim to please," Alicia said.

"You know, the potential for our business really is limitless," Jamie said when they were once again blissfully alone. "We could make some sort of discount-coupon book for all the great deals we get around town."

"I'm already getting a commercial discount at the fabric store," Carmen said.

Jamie held up her thumb and index finger and said, "We're *this close* to having a *quince* empire."

As the friends laughed, the bell rang. Grabbing her books, Alicia said, "And I'm *this* close to failing organic chemistry. I love being the queen of *quince*, but it's a full-time job."

"*Ay*, don't mention the word *fail*," Carmen said. "I wanted to go to the library to research traditional Mexican costumes for dress ideas. But I've got to use my study hall to write a draft of my American history paper. See you *chicas* later."

Carmen gave her girls a quick hug and took off down the south hallway. Like many historic buildings in South Florida, C. G. High was a one-story art deco building with big windows, white walls, and large open spaces. The halls were lined with brightly lit display cases. Some were filled with trophies won by the school's varsity football team, the Cavaliers. Others featured writing and artwork from the senior literary magazine, *Catharsis*, or solicitations for donations for school supplies for C.G.'s sister school in the Dominican Republic.

"I'm going to life drawing," Jamie said to Alicia. "I'll walk you to the science class."

As the girls made their way down the hall they were greeted by other students.

"Nice party last weekend," a girl with red hair called out.

"Thanks," Alicia and Jamie said in unison.

"Yo, Gaz said he'd burn me a CD of those tracks he played at Katerina's *quince*," a boy in a C.G. letter jacket called out. "Tell him it's for Gary."

"I will," Alicia said.

Jamie grinned. "It's kind of cool, isn't it?"

"What?"

"It's like we're famous," Jamie said.

A group of girls who had attended Carmen's multiculti Lati-Jew-na *quince* honoring her mixed Jewish and Latino heritage walked by and held up the spray-painted bags that Jamie had made for their best friend's celebration. "*Hola y* shalom," the girls called out, using the Spanish and Hebrew words for *hello* that Jamie had tagged in block-print graffiti on the front and back of each guest's stylish party favor. Jamie laughed. "You see what I mean?"

Alicia had to agree. In their corner of the world, there was no doubt they really were almost famous. Life, it would seem, couldn't get much sweeter.

CHAPTER 2

LATER THAT AFTERNOON, Alicia sat
at the kitchen table of the Cruz home looking wistfully
at the family pool. She had a five-page paper to write
about Rigoberta Menchú, a fascinating woman and
Nobel Prize–winner from Guatemala who had been a
worldwide advocate for the rights of her native Mayan
people. Despite the plethora of material, Alicia was
not feeling inspired. Maybe, just maybe, a quick swim
would help clear her head.

She got up from the table and began to imagine the
cool, fresh water of the pool on her back when a voice
stopped her. "Sweetie, stay focused."

Turning around, she saw that Maribelle had come
to stand in the doorway. In her hands, she held grocery
bags.

Alicia walked over, welcoming the distraction. How
could Maribelle argue if the procrastination helped

her? She began to unpack the groceries.

"What's for dinner?" she asked.

"I thought I would do a ceviche with scallops and cod."

"Did I hear the word *ceviche*?" Alicia's mother said as she walked into the room. She kicked off her shoes, a pair of mock-crocodile platform pumps that Alicia had coveted from the moment that her mother had bought them.

Marisol Cruz was one of Miami's toughest judges, and she dressed the part. Her designer suits and power dresses were always courtroomworthy. Alicia saw herself more as a creative type. Her fashion sense was as keen as her mother's, but it reflected a more bohemian sense of style and attitude that always worked with Alicia's dark eyes, flawless skin, and wavy brown hair.

That wasn't to say that she wasn't organized—and sometimes, in fact, even seemed to have borderline OCD. She handled everything for Amigas Inc., from choreography to coming up with ideas for set designs that were often executed by Alex, her handsome older brother, who was an aspiring architecture student.

Now, as Alicia looked at her mom, barefoot in a charcoal gray sheath with a lovely draped cowl neck, she thought, not for the first time, that even if they weren't similar now, she wouldn't mind growing up to be like her mother. When she was handling the business end of things, Alicia already enjoyed stepping out of her I'm-a-creative-artist box and doing a Marisol Cruz imitation. She brought to the job that fierce combination of capability and intelligence that had made her mom a star, even during her days at Harvard Law School.

Unaware of her daughter's silent appraisal, Marisol Cruz kissed Maribelle on each cheek, European-style, then came over and gave her only daughter a big hug. "¿Qué pasa, niña?" she asked. "How's it going with Rigoberta Menchú?"

"Don't ask," Alicia said, groaning. "I'm having a really hard time concentrating. I feel like my brain is flipping back and forth between a hundred things at once. How do you keep yourself on track, *Mami*?"

"Not easily," laughed her mother. "I have a lot of notes and a lot of reminders, and sometimes, I don't focus as well as I'd like. It's part of being human."

"I guess," Alicia said. "But still . . ." Her voice trailed off as the smell of cooking filled the room.

Maribelle had begun to make fresh tortilla chips. Cutting the small flour tortillas into quarters, she then plopped them into the cast-iron pan, in which sizzled canola oil. The moment she took the first batch of tortillas out of the pan, Alicia grabbed one and popped it in her mouth.

"Let it cool!" Maribelle warned.

"But they're so good when they're hot," Alicia countered, grabbing another.

"I couldn't agree more," her mother said, reaching for her own chip.

Maribelle shooed them both away. "Out of my kitchen! The salsa is not even made yet, and there will be no more chips at the rate you two are going."

Alicia and her mother laughed but did as they were told. Food was a shared passion in the Cruz household, and that meant following Maribelle's strict, albeit tender, rules.

Mrs. Cruz joined Alicia at the kitchen table, where Maribelle had put out a fresh pitcher of lemonade. She poured her daughter a glass and then poured one for herself.

"So, I know I should be letting you get back to your paper. You know how I *hate* to interrupt you while you're doing your schoolwork. . . ." Marisol began.

"Please, please, interrupt me," Alicia begged her.

Marisol chuckled. "Well, if you insist. I was just wondering if you've given any thought to spring break."

Alicia hadn't. In fact, she, Carmen, Jamie, and Gaz

had been so busy planning *quinces*, keeping up with their schoolwork, and making time for their relationships that they'd totally forgotten about spring break. It wasn't until one of their customers mentioned plans to take a trip to Key West that they all remembered.

"It's a complete bummer," Alicia said. "We've been working so hard, and for once we all have a little money socked away. But Jamie's checked everything out, and we've got nothing, nada to look forward to while we're on vacation. All of the best concerts are sold out. The beaches and Bongos will be filled with partying college students. Our current plan was to get some great books, check into Club Cruz, and do the one thing there is to do in Miami during spring break if you don't want to end up in somebody's embarrassing homemade YouTube video or worse—stay cool, perfect your backstroke, and hang out by the pool."

"Does Club Cruz mean I cook for you and all your friends?" Maribelle asked, bringing over a bowl of the tortilla chips and a cup of homemade salsa.

Alicia dipped a chip and smiled. "Only if we're very lucky."

"You got that right," Maribelle said.

"Well, I've got another offer, if you're interested," her mother said mysteriously.

Alicia raised an eyebrow and waited.

"Do you remember my old law school friend Ranya?"

"Not really," Alicia replied. "But go on."

"Ranya's at a law firm in Austin, Texas, and she's got a daughter, Valeria, who is just about your age," Alicia's mom explained. "I sent her the write-up that the *Miami Herald* did on you and Amigas Inc., and she was very impressed."

Alicia smiled at the pride she detected in her mother's voice. The summer before, when she had decided to form Amigas Incorporated, her mother had been her most vocal critic—worrying that a party-planning business was not a serious venture for her daughter. But once she had attended the first *quince* that Amigas planned, she realized that the company's goal to create a *quinceañera* that was more than just a party, but a celebration of a culture and a time-honored tradition welcoming Latina girls into womanhood, was a good one.

As the business grew and the company began to receive not only more customers than they could handle, but also coverage from local newspapers and TV, Marisol Cruz grew even prouder. By the time Amigas Inc. was featured in the *Miami Herald*, she was a hundred percent behind the business. She even had seventy-five copies of the article from the paper printed up and sent to her friends and colleagues across the country.

Mrs. Cruz reached into her bag and pulled out a copy of the article. "Do you remember what they wrote?" she asked. Alicia nodded. Ignoring her daughter's nod, Mrs. Cruz began reading from the article: *". . . These bright and resourceful teenagers are masters of the cultural mash-up. The* quinceañeras *they plan are an effortless mix of the modern and the traditional."*

"*¡Mamacita, por favor!* You've read that article a gazillion times!" Alicia protested halfheartedly. She always pretended to be blasé about it, but kept a copy of the same article in her handbag—a red leather barrel that had been a hand-me-down.

"Okay, okay. I'll stop. But the point is, Ranya's daughter, Valeria, is turning fifteen, and she would like to fly you and your business partners over to Austin to plan her party during your spring break."

Her mother had to be kidding, right? No. She couldn't be. She wouldn't mess with her daughter about something like this.

Jumping up, Alicia did a little victory dance. "Woo-hoo!" Then she stopped. "Okay, wait," she said.

"I need details. Is there a catch?"

Her mother shook her head. "All I know is, Ranya's done very well for herself, and her husband's family is in the oil business. She wrote me that Valeria is a little shy and introverted and that sometimes she has to ask her to speak up just to hear her at the dinner table." She paused as she grabbed another chip. Alicia crossed her arms and waited. Noting her daughter's anxious look, Marisol went on. "So, Ranya spent months interviewing dozens of local party-planners and knew they would all torture Valeria by insisting on a Texas-size party and a poufy white dress. She told me that Valeria is very proud of her Tex-Mex culture and wanted to honor it in a way that felt personal—and appropriate for her, not what a planner thought would be right. The family had decided they would have a small, intimate gathering.

"But when Ranya showed Valeria the profile of Amigas Inc., she got excited," Marisol continued. "She thought you guys would be able to deliver the kind of party she wanted and told her mom that, with your help, she'd be excited to have a big celebration. According to Ranya, that's a *huge* step."

Alicia clapped her hands. "Spring break has been saved! You're even more of a genius than I thought you were." She grabbed her phone off the table. "Who should I call first? Gaz? Carmen? Jamie?"

"Aren't you forgetting something? What about your Rigoberta Menchú paper?" her mother asked, holding up the art book Alicia had been referencing.

"I'll focus on that all weekend long. I promise. But right now, I've got to let my partners know that we're taking the *quince* act on the road."

With her mother's laughing permission, Alicia went and sprawled on the chaise longue near the living room's sliding-glass door. She punched seven digits into the phone. No answer. She hung up.

"Ugh! I totally forgot," she said to no one in particular. "Jamie's having dinner with the Mortimers at the club." She hoped that this dinner was going to be less dramatic than the first dinner Jamie had attended at the country club. In an attempt to make a statement, she had worn a ridiculous outfit and almost cost Amigas Inc. a huge job and almost cost herself a relationship with Dash.

Alicia figured that Jamie was doing just fine as she didn't use the ringing cell phone as an excuse to leave the table.

She punched another number into the phone. Again, no answer. "And Carmen is taking that class in fashion illustration at the New World School for the Arts."

She hung up and dialed again. Finally, someone answered. "Gaz?" she said excitedly when her boy-friend picked up. "You're *never* going to believe who our next customer is. I'm telling you, Amigas Inc. is blowing up!"

"Is it another hard-to-please heiress like Binky? I'm sorry, I mean Bianca?" Gaz asked playfully. They had given her a hard time, but the whole group loved Binky Mortimer. She was OTT but a huge sweetheart.

"As far as I know, she's nothing like our worst cases. She's rich, but she's not an heiress, she doesn't have a Jewish grandma intent on running the show her way, and the gig doesn't involve a TV reality show," Alicia replied. "So what are you doing now?"

"Not much," said Gaz. "Have anything interesting in mind?"

"I have something delicious in mind," replied Alicia. "Come over for dinner. I'll fill you in on all the details of our new gig."

Alicia put her hand over the mouthpiece, then called out, "Hey, Maribelle! Can Gaz come over to dinner?"

"Fine with me," Maribelle yelled back. "I could never say no to my biggest fan. But you have to ask your mother."

Alicia cried: "*Mami*, can—"

"Fine with me," her mother chimed in before Alicia could finish.

Just then, Alicia's father and brother walked in.

Enrique Cruz was in his early fifties, with the lithe build of a guy who'd spent his entire childhood playing soccer and still spent weekends chasing the soccer ball up and down the field. Dressed in a casual business outfit consisting of a deep turquoise polo shirt and dark khakis, he looked more businessman than athlete tonight. Alex was dressed in his usual attire, a white polo shirt, tan khakis, and loafers with no socks. "Hey, Dad, you know the funny thing about when it's just the women at home? The house is *so* quiet."

"I completely agree," Alicia's father said, laughing.

"*¡Cállate la boca!*" Alicia, her mother, and Maribelle cried out in unison.

Alicia quickly told Gaz to come on over, hung up, and ran upstairs and grabbed her laptop. She wanted to do some research on Texas ASAP.

"Oh, good," Marisol said, seeing the laptop tucked under her arm. "You should check your e-mail. Ranya said Valeria was going to try and shoot you a note. Maybe she got to it."

Alicia sat down at the kitchen table and logged on.

Sure enough, there was an e-mail waiting for her from Valeria:

Hi Alicia: Hopefully by now your mom has told you all about my crazy dream of getting Amigas Inc. over to Texas to help me plan my party! And hopefully, you are all on board. I would LOVE if you came. I know the deadline is tight . . .

Alicia stopped reading and looked up at her mother. "Tight deadline?" she asked. "How tight?"

Marisol shrugged. "I think you've done *quinces* in less time, but Ranya does want it to happen at the end of spring break, so you have two weeks."

The color momentarily drained from Alicia's face. She took a deep breath. They could do this. Her mother was right. They'd had less time in the past and made it work. Turning back to her e-mail, she continued to read:

So I wanted to give you a heads-up in advance about my taste. Black is my color of choice; I don't do frills and am allergic to the color pink. My iPod is filled with tunes by local Austin indie artists like Roger Velasquez. I have a bangin' collection of vintage graphic novels from the eighties. As for food, I think its gross to eat anything that was once a living thing. I'm into line dancing but only as an observer. I have no dance skills whatsoever. I love to skateboard and my happiest times are cruising down the half-pipe at the Austin County skate park. Our homestead, Castillo Ranch, is my favorite place in the world. Oh, and I usually like to get right to the point. Hope this is some help. See you soon. Valeria.

Although Ranya had described her daughter as being painfully shy, Alicia thought she was impressive. From her writing it seemed as though she had the confidence to know exactly what she wanted and, more to the point, exactly what she didn't. This was going to make for one very interesting party.

Half an hour later, Gaz arrived at the Cruz home. He kissed Alicia on the forehead, then hugged Maribelle and Alicia's mom. Alicia loved the easy interaction he had with her family. She knew girls whose parents disapproved of the guys they were dating. They could only see each other at school or when they managed to sneak a few moments at a movie or a house party. With Gaz, there were no such problems. She could see him whenever she wanted—no sneaking around necessary.

Sometimes, in fact, Alicia was pretty sure her

parents liked Gaz more than they liked her! Well, not more, but close.

Her parents didn't always approve of the things she liked. But she could tell that when her parents looked at Gaz, they saw what she saw—a smart, handsome guy, who was proud of his Latino heritage and had the potential to do anything he set his mind to.

Still, Alicia *was* her daddy's girl. So even if he liked Gaz, Enrique took great pleasure in grilling the younger man about his future whenever he came over to the house. Gaz, for his part, was respectful and formal, going along with the gentle ribbing. While Gaz called Alicia's mom by her first name, he called her father Señor Cruz.

Now, over plates of ceviche, Alicia's father played twenty questions with Gaz.

"What's your toughest class this year?"

"Definitely statistics," Gaz replied as he tucked in heartily to his meal.

"What about algebra two?" Alicia's father asked. "Don't you need that to get into a good college?"

Alicia put a hand on her father's. "Gaz took algebra two last year, *Papi*. He was the only freshman in the class. His math skills are off the hook. You know that."

Enrique raised an eyebrow. "Off the hook, huh? What are you pulling in statistics?"

Gaz helped himself to a pile of *plátanos*. "A minus. It's a really hard class."

"Do you think you can pull it up to an A by the final?" Mr. Cruz asked, taking the plate from Gaz and shoveling the remaining sweet plantains onto his own dish.

"That's the goal, sir." Gaz smiled.

"Good," Alicia's father said. "You keep me posted on how that's going."

When dinner—and the questions—were done, Gaz and Alicia cleared the table and then went into the kitchen together and cleaned up. The extra help meant that Maribelle could nip out to the Florida room to watch her favorite *telenovela*.

As they loaded the last dishes into the washer, Alicia turned to Gaz with a playful smile. "Do you have time for a swim?"

He grinned back. "Always. I even brought my suit."

She went to her room to change while Gaz changed in the half bathroom off the kitchen. As they walked out to the pool together, Alicia instinctively reached for his hand, surprised anew at just how right it felt. She wondered if it would ever stop giving her butterflies—holding his hand, seeing how handsome he was, like now, in his papaya-colored board shorts that showed off his natural tan perfectly.

She stood near the edge of the pool, preparing herself for the jump into the cool water, when Gaz surprised her. Grabbing her by the waist, he jumped into the water taking her with him. She screamed and laughed as they both plunged under.

"Hey!" she said, pretending to be miffed as she surfaced and spluttered. "What's the big idea?"

Gaz didn't answer. He just kissed her, the kind of kiss that made her quiver, as if she were made of jello.

"That's the big idea," he said, when he finally disconnected his lips from hers.

"I like it," she smiled. "I also like the idea of us in Austin, all expenses paid, for spring break. Aren't you excited?"

"I am excited," Gaz sighed, sounding anything but. "And I love that Amigas Inc. has taken off. It's just a bummer that the trip is at the same time as the yearly South by Southwest Music and Media Conference in Austin, but by now, the tickets are completely sold out. It's sucky timing. I mean, if I had known, I could've gone. I've always dreamed about going to South by Southwest. It has all kinds of cutting-edge media presentations, music showcases, and film screenings. It's the place to be if you want to get exposure and buzz going for your work. Watching you rock the *quince* business in Miami makes me want to take my music to the next level. But I don't know. I'm just not as good at putting myself out there as you are."

Alicia hated to hear Gaz criticize himself. She kissed him lightly. "You're an amazing songwriter. You pour your entire soul into every song."

"But if I'm going to be a successful musician, I'm going to have to learn how to *sell* my music. I want to turn on the radio and hear my songs. I want to play stadiums, like Coldplay, or even minor-league baseball stadiums, like Wilco. I want to go all the way, and I don't even know where to start," Gaz insisted, ignoring his girlfriend's support. "There's *so* much I could learn at a place like South by Southwest."

"So, we'll get you a ticket," Alicia said.

"How?" Gaz asked.

Alicia beamed at her boyfriend. "I'll make a way out of no way. It's my thing."

Gaz pulled her close, hugging her tight. "It's enough that you are trying. That you just believe in me."

Alicia hugged him back. "I do believe in you, Gaz."

"I know you do," he said. "And that makes a world of difference. With you by my side, I can do anything."

CHAPTER 3

THAT NIGHT, AFTER Gaz left, Alicia was too excited to sleep. She had managed to get ahold of Carmen and Jamie earlier and filled them in. But they were still waiting to get the okay from their folks. Figuring that chatting was better than tossing and turning, she logged on to her computer and joined a group chat with her girls.

Alicia:	What's the dealio? Any word?
Carmen:	My mom says she has 2 talk 2 your mom.
Alicia:	Tell her 2 call now. She's still up.
	Remind them—mom is chaperoning!
	We'll behave!
Jamie:	I'm going to Austin!!! Dad said okay.
Alicia:	Cool. Da Amigas are heading to the Lone Star State!
Carmen:	Good news + bad news.

Alicia: Bad news first.

Carmen: Domingo can't come. He's got 2 work.

Alicia: But you're coming. That's awesome.

Carmen: Gonna miss him though.

Alicia: It's just two weeks.

Carmen: Says the only girl whose guy is coming.

Jamie: True that. Dash has got a golf tournament.

Alicia: Trying to get Gaz 2 music festival in Austin. He'll be busy @ nite. Girls will hang.

Carmen: Absence makes the heart grow fonder, right?

Jamie: It's working for me and Dash. No time 2 argue. He travels so much on the golf circuit when he comes home, we just chill and have fun.

Carmen: Gonna miss Domingo soooooo much.

Jamie: Text him every day.

Alicia: Write him real letters. More romantic.

Jamie: Buy him a cowboy hat.

Carmen: :^)

Alicia: We'll buy all our guys cowboy hats.

Jamie: Preppy Dash in a ten gallon hat. Hi-larious.

Alicia: I'm fading. Got 2 go.

Carmen: Ciao for now.

Jamie: Later, ladies.

As soon as classes let out the Friday of spring break, the members of Amigas Inc. rushed to their various homes to pack for their trip. Their flight was early the next morning, and they were going to be together for two weeks, but before the fun could start, there was just so much to do!

Alicia paced her room. Her mother had treated her to a brand-new suitcase—a leopard-print hardcase with a hot pink interior. It was huge, so Alicia knew it would hold everything she needed. The problem was that she had no idea *what* to bring. The pile of neglected clothes sat in a big mound on the floor. The suitcase itself was empty, except for her toothbrush.

This was an emergency. She decided to call Carmen for some expert advice.

"Carmen, I don't know what to pack!" Alicia cried, cradling the phone between her ear and shoulder. "You're the fashion genius; I'm drowning here, and I desperately need your help."

In Carmen's room, a silver vinyl duffel bag sat fully packed and ready to go by the door. Besides being a kick-butt fashion designer, Carmen had been blessed with the genetic ability to pack both lightly *and* fashionably—without even trying. Her suitcase was like the ones you saw in fashion-magazine articles, where seven items morphed magically into twenty-one different outfits.

"Well, it'll be cooler in Austin than it is in Miami, especially at night," said Carmen calmly. "So, plan to layer."

Alicia, who was dressed in a black miniskirt, cream-colored sleeveless sweater, and black pearl necklace, shook her head. "Come on, *chica*, you know I don't do layers. I do miniskirts and cute tops."

Carmen laughed.

"Hold on, I'm getting another call," Carmen said. She switched lines. It was Jamie.

Jamie was standing in her own bedroom staring miserably into her vintage steamer trunk, which was empty except for a set of watercolor paints, her sketch-book, and a toothbrush.

"Carmen, you gotta help me out!" Jamie cried. "I don't know what to pack."

"Not you, too," Carmen said. "I love you ladies, but you have got to get it together!"

"Come pack for me," Jamie begged her. "I'll give you this cool vintage dress I just scored on eBay."

Carmen's eyes lit up. Jamie was the queen of vin-tage finds; from the thrift stores of Miami Beach to the coolest Japanese vendors on eBay, the world was just a treasure chest of goodies waiting for Jamie to find them.

"New or used?" Carmen asked, interested.

"Mint condition," Jamie replied. "But I guess you'll have to come over and check it out for yourself."

"My size?" Carmen asked. She was model thin and nearly six feet tall, which meant that not everything that fit her friends looked good on her.

"Your size," Jamie said.

That was all it took.

"I'll be over in twenty minutes," Carmen promised.

She hung up the phone, and it immediately started ringing again. Alicia! Carmen had completely forgotten she was on the other line.

"Sorry, *chica*," Carmen said. "Jamie and I were talking eBay finds."

"This is no time for eBay!" Alicia shouted, still pacing the room. Carmen could hear her kitten heels click-clack-click on the floor.

"Come pack for me," Alicia begged her. "It's our first Amigas Inc. trip, and I've got to bring my A game."

Carmen laughed, mostly because the idea of Alicia's bringing less than her A game was so ridiculous. They didn't call her Type A Alicia for nothing.

"Well, Jamie just offered me a vintage treasure to

come and help *her* pack," Carmen said. "What you got, *chica*, to make me come to your house, too?"

Alicia raised an eyebrow. "How about my unending friendship, my deepest loyalty, and my most profound respect?"

Carmen giggled. "Throw in a plate of Maribelle's empanadas and you've got yourself a deal."

"Done! See you soon!"

On the other end of the line, Carmen shrugged. "Just don't blame me if Jamie complains I didn't spend enough time on her."

Alicia nodded on the other end. "I'll take the heat. Now enough talking. Get over here. The clock is ticking!"

At seven the next morning, they all met up at Miami International Airport. Their flight didn't leave until nine, but check-in began two hours before, and Alicia's mom liked to be on the early side. She had told everyone else's parents to do the same.

Thanks to Carmen's wardrobe consultations, each of the female members of Amigas Inc. were not only efficiently packed, with one carry-on suitcase each, they were also perfectly dressed for the trip in cute and comfy leggings, long, embroidered T-shirts, and airplane-friendly cashmere wraps. Gaz carried an impossibly small duffel bag and wore his standard uniform: jeans, a blue cotton button-down shirt, and old-school high-tops.

Even after Carmen had visited both Jamie and Alicia to help them pack, the three girls had stayed up texting until almost two in the morning. As they'd gotten a grand total of about four hours of sleep, they greeted one another with yawns and sleepy whispers.

Gaz, on the other hand, was wide awake and raring to go. He was so pumped about the South by Southwest Festival that at one point, before he could be stopped, *and* much to Alicia's chagrin, he jumped on a chair in the airport lounge and screamed, "We're going to Austin, everybody! The home of the indie music scene."

He was only a little embarrassed when Alicia's mother motioned for him to get down and said, "No more coffee for you, Gaz." There was no way his mood was getting dimmed. Not even by a calling-out. Or the prospect of a long flight with Alicia giving him the cold shoulder for embarrassing her.

Luckily, once they got on the plane, the trip went smoothly, and exactly two hours and forty minutes later, and three bags of M&M's, eight sodas, a lot of pea-nuts, and one teeny-tiny incident involving a mixed-up seating assignment, the plane touched down in Texas, where everything—including the *quinceañeras*—was bigger. It was time to start planning—once they found their ride.

"Let's head to baggage claim," Mrs. Cruz suggested when everyone was safely off the plane and accounted for. "Ranya said she would meet us there."

Turning, she led the group, like a mother duckling, through the terminal, following signs to the baggage claim. After what felt longer than the flight itself, they made it.

And boy, was it a sight.

Crowds of people dressed like extras in a Western, with cowboy hats, leather boots, and big belt buckles, looked for their loved ones.

Ranya was easy to find, though. She was holding a sign that read: TEXAS LOVES YOU, AMIGAS INC.!

Valeria, or the girl Alicia assumed was Valeria, stood behind her. She was wearing a pair of black combat boots, graffiti-print leggings, and a T-shirt that said, KEEP AUSTIN WEIRD. Her eyes were hidden beneath bushy eyebrows, and her pale face was framed by hair that could only be referred to as a wild mess, except for one braid that dangled over her left eye.

From the way her mother was jumping up and

down while Valeria hung back, slouching and looking embarrassed, there seemed little doubt as to who had made the sign and was most excited about the *quince*.

Alicia was frankly surprised. From the e-mails they'd exchanged, Valeria had seemed very sure of herself, but maybe that was not the case after all.

Leaving the others, she walked up to the girl. "Hi! I'm Alicia. It's great to finally meet you. I feel like we should already know each other! We're really honored to be planning your *quince*."

"*Mucho gusto*, Alicia," Valeria said softly. "I read the newspaper articles, and I have to give you Miami girls so much respect. As I wrote in my e-mail, I'm not much of a party girl, but the *quince* tradition means a great deal to my family and me, and I'm depending on you to help me throw a party which honors our tradition and makes us proud."

Alicia, who knew better than to judge a book by its cover, was impressed by Valeria's graciousness. She nodded. "That we can do. I have a few questions I forgot to ask over e-mail. . . ." As she began to throw ideas and questions out, the group members began to make their way to the conveyor belt that had just started moving, indicating the arrival of their bags. The moms chatted while Jamie and Carmen sent texts to their boys, and

Gaz searched on his phone for SXSW info.

"Let me guess," Ranya said, turning her attention from Marisol to Gaz. "I take it you're a musician."

"How'd you know?" he asked.

"Well, the guitar strapped to your back was a pretty big clue," Ranya said, laughing.

Gaz looked a bit embarrassed and reached behind to pat his guitar. "Do you know I actually forget that I've got it on? Incredible."

"Well, your timing couldn't be better. We're having a huge music festival and conference here in Austin."

"South by Southwest," Gaz said, nodding. "Everybody knows about it. But I also know everything is sold out."

"Well, you don't need tickets to get in on the scene," Ranya said. "Every barbecue spot, coffeehouse, and restaurant is going to be turned into a juke joint this week. There's going to be music everywhere."

Alicia, caught up in *quince* details with Valeria, hadn't been listening, but she perked up when she heard talk of the conference. "Sounds like fun," she said, "but Gaz is going to be up to his eyeballs getting all the music together for your *quince*. He's not going to have a minute of free time to just hang out."

"She's the boss." Gaz chuckled, though he didn't

look exactly thrilled. "But I bet you could already tell that."

Alicia gave him a playful swat on the arm. "Gaz teases me for being a *mandona*," she pouted, "but he knows how much pressure it is to get a *quince* up and running. Speaking of the *quince*, Valeria, I'm so sorry I've been hogging you. Let me introduce you to the rest of the team."

Going one by one, she made the intros. "This is Carmen," she said. "She's our resident dress designer, seamstress, and all-around-quiet-in-the-midst-of-any-*quince*-storm member."

Valeria flicked her long, pin-straight, jet black hair away from her face shyly and waved at Carmen. Carmen waved back and, with a big smile, said, "Nice to meet you, Valeria, I'm looking forward to working with you."

"I'm Jamie Sosa," Jamie said before Alicia could introduce her. "I'm the AV department of Amigas Inc. Everything from oil painting to digital video, I'm your girl."

"Hi," Valeria said. "Cool sneakers. Aren't those from Tokyo?"

"Whoa," Jamie said, clearly impressed. "How'd you know that?"

"I have a little skateboard sneaker collection," Valeria replied. "Not many, but I love each and every pair."

"*Mija*, that's a sure sign that you and I are going to get along just fine," Jamie said enthusiastically. "I'm a complete and total sneaker freak. I bet your sneaker stash is amazing."

After Gaz said his hellos, they gathered up their various bags. "Okay, you all," Ranya said, clapping her hands and bringing everyone to attention. "We need to get this party on the road."

Because they were such a big group, two of the ranch managers had driven out to meet the Miami crew at the airport. From the moment the Castillo Ranch vans rolled out of the Austin city limits and onto the I-35, the group was unusually silent. They'd heard about the Texas plains—and seen them, on TV at least. In an effort to "*pre*-prepare," Jamie had insisted that they watch half a dozen independent films set in Texas. But it was different seeing it up close. Miami was all art deco architecture mixed with sleek high-rises, surrounded by the glitz of South Beach, the majestic expanse of the ocean, and all of the lush island flora. Texas, by comparison, was like an Andrew Wyeth painting—rolling hills, knee-high grass, hundred-year-old oaks, and Huck Finn–worthy streams.

When the sound of growling stomachs began to fill the van, Valeria texted her mother, who was riding in the other van with Marisol, to suggest that the group stop for lunch. The Miami guests had been traveling since early morning, and their stomachs could attest to the fact that they were hungry.

"I need a nap," Gaz said, nodding. "But I need food more than sleep."

"Well, this place is right down the road from the ranch, and it has what the Austin locals think is the best barbecue in Texas," Valeria said.

Gaz sat up and rubbed his hands together. "I'll take your best barbecue, thank you very much. Then I'll take seconds."

Ninety minutes later, despite the beautiful surroundings, the Miami natives were starting to get officially cranky and restless.

"Where the heck are we?" Jamie muttered.

"This is hill country," Valeria replied, turning around in the front passenger seat to face her. "Isn't it beautiful?"

"What it is," Jamie said, "is far. I thought you said we were going someplace nearby."

"Oh, Driftwood's not far," Valeria said. "We should be there any minute."

"But we've been driving for nearly two hours," Alicia said, whining just a little.

"You gotta remember. It's a big state on a big swath of land. It takes some time to get from place to place." Then Valeria looked out the window and smiled. "See? We're here!"

"Here" was the Salt Lick Barbecue Restaurant. And it was, to put it mildly, a far cry from the group's favorite Miami hangout, Bongos. Bongos was in the heart of South Beach, on elegant Ocean Drive. The furniture was upholstered in bright tropical patterns, and giant palm trees framed the ocean views outside the floor-to-ceiling windows.

The Salt Lick was all outdoors, and all casual. Cooks dressed in kitchen whites tended a giant open barbecue pit, and dozens of people crowded the rustic property, enjoying their meals on weathered wooden picnic tables.

"I hope you like it," Valeria said. "It's a huge family favorite."

Standing in the parking lot, looking at the muddy grass fields, the three girls took a moment to consider their footwear. Alicia was wearing mules with two inch heels. Carmen was wearing a pair of sand-colored designer espadrilles, and Jamie, like the majority of the

Salt Lick customers, was wearing boots. But Jamie's boots were made of a very light butter-colored suede that would have been ruined by one trek across the field.

"Is there a paved walkway to the tables?" Carmen asked, voicing the concern of all of them. "I hate to seem overly citified. But these are my favorite espadrilles, and it took me almost a year to save for them."

Valeria, who was wearing a pair of perfectly broken-in red cowboy boots, politely stifled a giggle. "A walkway? You are kidding, right?"

Alicia's mother, still talking animatedly to Valeria's mother, bounded past them. Gaz followed, as if he were being pulled by an invisible barbecue string, with a big, silly, feed-me-now grin on his face.

The girls stood in the parking lot, torn between the growling in their bellies and the incredible smell of slow-cooked ribs wafting from the open pit, and the very real consideration that they were each about to ruin their favorite shoes, shoes they'd worn with the intention of looking fierce, fabulous, and flawless while visiting a new city.

Then a table opened up near the parking lot, and Valeria grabbed it; it was now or never. Ever so daintily, they tiptoed across the ground, holding their breath.

To strangers, they probably looked anything but fierce. Instead, they looked like timid cats near water.

"Oh, wow," Valeria said, when the girls made it to the table, breathing heavy sighs of relief as they sat down, shoes somehow unscathed. "I hope you brought more practical footwear for the rest of your trip."

"My other shoes are sandals," Alicia said.

"My other shoes are pumps," Carmen said.

"We've got to get you *chicas* boots," Valeria said.

"But I *am* wearing boots," Jamie pointed out.

Valeria shook her head. "Real boots. *Cowboy* boots."

Before she could further assess—or diss—their footwear, a waitress in a blue and white gingham shirt and jeans looped around their table, passing out menus, glasses of ice water, and baskets of warm corn bread.

"So, what do you recommend here?" Carmen asked turning to her host. "Everything smells so good."

Valeria's hair was in her face again, and she distractedly pushed it to the side. "By all accounts, all the meat is good," she said quietly. "But I can't really advise you, because I'm a vegetarian."

Alicia had mentioned this to Jamie back in Miami, after receiving Valeria's first e-mail. Even so, Jamie looked a bit surprised, as if it just didn't seem possible. "That must be hard, living in a place where meat being simmered over a campfire is the norm."

Valeria smiled. "Actually, it's sort of just the opposite. Seeing how closely people here are tied to the land, I respect the fact that many of the people I know don't eat meat carelessly. They know and care for the animals."

A few minutes later, the girls watched as she happily dug in to a platter of potato salad, mustard greens, and baked beans that the waitress had provided.

Jamie, who'd ordered a side of greens with her ribs, took a bite and then groaned happily. "These greens are more delicious than any leafy vegetable has the right to be."

Alicia nodded, her mouth full. When she finally swallowed, she added, "These are the best baked beans I've ever had in my whole entire life." Then she paused. "No one tell Maribelle I said that."

Valeria laughed. "All of the vegetables here are cooked with huge slabs of pork. That's what gives them so much flavor. Technically, the veggies here aren't vegetarian at all. But I make an exception whenever I come to the Lick."

For the rest of the meal, the group focused only on eating. After the flight, and with the time difference, they were all a little worn out. But they had to admit, it was nice to hang out in the fresh air and listen to the chatter around them.

Later, as they walked—make that *waddled*—toward the vans, Valeria leaned in toward her mom. "We've got to take the girls shopping for some boots," she said in a stage whisper. "All they've got is fancy high-heeled shoes."

"I heard that," laughed Alicia's mother. Turning to her daughter, she said, "With all the drama you put into packing, I can't believe you girls didn't bring practical shoes."

"I blame Carmen, she packed for me," Jamie said playfully.

"Hey, watch it," Carmen warned.

"I also blame Carmen," Alicia said, winking at Jamie. "She was my wardrobe supervisor as well."

"Guess it's lucky I'm a big boy," joked Gaz. "I picked out my clothes and packed for myself. And I'm the only one who can get mud on my shoes and not freak out."

"You *chicas*!" Carmen laughed. "So ungrateful! Don't come looking for me in two weeks, when you're desperately trying to fit your ten-gallon hat and all of your spring-break shopping into one teeny-weeny suitcase."

"She has a point," Alicia said, "and we're bound to hear it from her at a later date. I'm sorry, Carmen."

"Feeling apologetic, Jamie?" Carmen asked. "It's not too late to beg for my forgiveness."

"Um, I'll pass," Jamie said. "I don't do Western chic, and I won't be buying a cowboy hat of any kind."

"Famous last words," Valeria said. "I don't mean to be pushy, but if I can give you one piece of advice as Texas newbies, save yourself a lot of time and heartache. Go ahead and embrace the hat."

Hats weren't the only way the members of Amigas Inc. knew they were definitely not in Miami anymore. When they finally pulled up to the ranch, their jaws collectively dropped. A forty-foot wrought-iron gate emblazoned with a giant cursive *C*, for Castillo, welcomed them onto the sprawling property. As they took in the view along the long driveway leading up to the main house, the girls—and even Gaz—oohed and aahed. Feeling goofy and just a little sleep-deprived, they waved at the grazing cows, the gaggles of geese, and the ornery-looking goats. When the van turned left and pulled up to the wooded area around the guesthouse where the Miami group would be staying, they clapped and cheered for the driver, Luis.

As they unloaded their bags from the back, the big Texas sky and the surrounding acres of cedar and oak trees seemed warm and inviting, as if they'd been dropped off at summer camp and each day ahead promised a new parcel of mystery, a new care package of fun.

CHAPTER 4

THE NEXT morning came all too quickly. After arriving the previous afternoon, the Miami crew had taken quick naps and then, at Ranya's orders, filed back into the vans to head into town—for cowboy boots. There was no way she would let them wander around the ranch in sandals, she explained. Of course, with three girls, all of whom prided themselves on being stylish no matter what the zip code, the shopping took a lot longer than Ranya might have expected. Three hours and roughly sixty pairs of rejected boots later, Alicia, Carmen, and Jamie all walked out of the store successful. By the time they got back to the ranch, they were officially wiped, and immediately headed to bed.

Ranya had left a note directing them to the big house for breakfast, but not everyone was ready at the same time. Jamie was the first—and she was hungry. As she walked outside, her nose was tickled by the smell of something amazing coming from the direction of the big house. She quickly made her way there.

When she walked into the huge kitchen, she found Valeria along with her mom and a man she assumed was Valeria's dad, cooking up a storm.

"We like to do a big breakfast on the ranch," Ranya called out over her shoulder. She was expertly manning numerous simmering pots on the giant six-burner stove.

"Especially on Sundays, when my dad is around to help," Valeria added, leaning her head on the man's shoulder.

"I'm David Castillo, or Dad," he said in a Southern twang, extending his hand. He was just a head taller than Valeria, with thick black curly hair and a slightly shy, slightly mischievous grin. Salsa *verde* whirled around inside the restaurant food processor he was using like a pro. "Welcome to Austin," he said.

There were big bay windows on each side of the kitchen, and through them Jamie could take in the ranch. On the drive over, Valeria had casually mentioned to the Miami crew that the ranch was big. *Ginormous* would have been a better word. At a thousand acres, with more than a dozen kinds of wildlife on the property, the Castillo family ranch seemed more like a national park than someone's home.

"Is there anything I can do to help?" Jamie asked, turning her attention back to her hosts.

"Oh, you shouldn't have said that," Valeria's father said, reaching into the fridge for a crate of eggs. "Now we're going to have to initiate you into the Castillo family breakfast club."

Jamie was never one to back down from a challenge. "Sounds like fun."

"Well, it *is* fun. *If* you successfully complete your task," David said cryptically.

Jamie looked at him curiously. "Sure, what is it?"

"*¡Migas!*" Valeria cried, tossing an egg to the startled Jamie, who just barely managed to catch it.

"*¡Migas!*" Ranya said, tossing another egg at her; she was more prepared this time and caught it easily.

"*¡Migas!*" David said, throwing yet another egg at her. Both he and Valeria collapsed in laughter when she failed to catch the last egg and it splattered against the tiled kitchen wall.

"What on earth . . . ?" a voice asked. Turning, Jamie saw that Alicia and her mother had entered the kitchen just in time to catch the tail end of the egg toss. Alicia looked perplexed, but Mrs. Cruz ran over and pulled her old friend into a bear hug.

"*¡Migas!*" she shouted happily.

As Jamie stood holding the eggs she'd caught, looking slightly shell-shocked, David wiped the egg goop off the wall. Valeria and her mother held their sides, laughing heartily.

"What's going on?" Alicia whispered to Jamie. "And what the heck are *migas*?"

Valeria wiped tears of laughter from her eyes and explained. "*Migas* are a Tejano specialty. Crispy tortillas. Fresh farm eggs. Chorizo, if you have it—which we do."

"Nopalitos, if you have them," Ranya added. "Which we do."

"Cotija cheese—" David began.

"If you have it," Alicia put in.

"Which I bet they do," Jamie grinned.

"We certainly do," David said. "And the tradition is, first Texas newbie down to breakfast gets to make the *migas* and compete for a prized spot in the Castillo family breakfast club."

"And I'm up for the challenge," Jamie said, grabbing a cast-iron pot from an overhead rack.

"Up for what?" Gaz asked as he bounded into the room.

"Jamie's taking the great *migas* breakfast challenge," Alicia said.

"The Amigas breakfast challenge?" Gaz asked, and everyone laughed.

By the time Carmen entered the kitchen and said, "What's going on?" no one would bother to explain.

Jamie cracked an egg into the sizzling hot pan and said simply, "Watch and learn."

Twenty minutes later, they all sat down to the most incredible breakfast feast that any of the Miami crew had ever seen—huevos rancheros with refried pintos and sliced avocado, yogurt with maple syrup and toasted *pepitas*, blue-corn muffins, turkey sausage, buttermilk biscuits, bacon, and, of course, Jamie's chorizo and *Cotija migas*. There were ten people in total around the table, but there was enough food for at least twenty more.

Before they could dig in, David held up Jamie's dish. "I must first taste the Amigas *migas*." He took a bite and chewed as everyone waited. "And I find them to be . . ."

He made a face and paused dramatically, and Jamie looked just a little worried. "*Muy sabroso*," he finally said. "Tasty. Senorita Sosa is now officially a member of the Castillo family breakfast club."

Everyone at the table clapped, and Jamie, always happy to step into the limelight, stood up and took a bow.

After that, there was just the sound of eating as everyone tackled the feast. "This is insane," Gaz said a while later, after polishing off what had to be his fifth buttermilk biscuit.

"Only if you mean *insane* as a synonym for *yum*," Alicia said, heaping another spoonful of salsa *verde* onto a tortilla.

"Breakfast is the most important meal of the day on a ranch," Valeria explained. "Everyone works such long hours, and even when your chore list is light, you want to be fueled for whatever the day may bring, be it a swim in the river or a seven-mile hike or haying an entire field."

At the mention of work, Carmen looked concerned. "We're not haying anything today, are we? Because I was planning to visit my cousin Yessy at UT Austin."

Jamie looked at her watch. "I've got to go in a little while, too. Dash set me up with a lesson with one of his pro friends at Barton Creek."

Valeria's father looked impressed. "Are you a golfer?"

"I'm working on it," Jamie said. "My boyfriend is big into golf, and I just started taking lessons. Before that, the closest I came to golf was watching *Tin Cup* on my portable DVD player."

"Do you get to play a lot with your boyfriend?" asked David.

"Not so much," Jamie replied. "Turns out playing golf with one of the top-ranked teen players in the country, even if he's your boyfriend, isn't so much fun."

"Well," David said, "I was planning on getting in a few holes today myself. I'll give you a ride over."

"I was hoping to score a pass to one of the workshops at South by Southwest," Gaz said. "Or, if I have no luck, spend the day at the Starbucks nearest to it, playing my guitar. Who knows? Maybe I'll meet a record exec who'll discover me and magically decide to sign me to his label. If only . . ." He sighed.

As everyone went through their plans, Alicia's face had been growing redder and redder. But she waited until Valeria, her parents, and her own mom left to completely lose it. "You guys, we are here to work, not socialize!" she fumed. "We've got a little over two weeks to pull this *quince* together from top to bottom. Valeria's family has flown us here at no small expense. We've got to do a stunning job."

"Chill, *chica*. I couldn't agree more," Jamie said. "Which is why I'll meet you back here—right after lunch."

Carmen nodded. "I'm all about it. Now that I've met

Valeria, I can work on sketches on the bus ride home. See you at four o'clock!"

Before Alicia could explain that neither of those options worked for her, Marisol returned to the kitchen with Ranya. They had made plans to visit the Blanton Museum of Art at the University of Texas to see a new exhibit on solar eclipses by a contemporary Mexican artist, Pablo Vargas Lugo.

"Lici, why don't you come with us to the museum?" her mom asked. "It should be a wonderful show."

"Solar eclipses. Can't wait. It sounds like a blast," Alicia replied, her voice dripping with sarcasm. "I think I'll take a pass and just hang out at the ranch. Maybe Valeria can show me around and we can spend the day together talking *quince* things. After all, somebody's got to stay focused."

CHAPTER 5

AFTER CARMEN, Jamie, and Gaz had gone their various ways and the moms had headed into town for a sightseeing trip, Valeria and Alicia were alone at the ranch.

"It's a gorgeous day," Valeria said. "I'll give you a tour of the property; I mean, if you'd like one. You ever ride a horse before?"

"It's, uh, been a while. But it's like riding a bike, right?" said Alicia, fibbing a little. She *had* ridden—once. She just hoped that some muscle memory of that lone, long ago elementary-school pony ride would kick in.

"Okay, then. I'm going to run up to the house and change. Do you want to change and I'll meet you back here, in, say, ten?"

"Sure," Alicia said, going upstairs to the guest room she was sharing with Jamie and Carmen.

She'd been wearing a cornflower blue sundress, a

red beaded necklace, and red sandals. A blue bandanna, folded as a headband, completed her country-chic look. But clearly, she couldn't go horseback riding in a dress. Alicia opened her suitcase and quickly changed into her favorite boot-cut jeans, a camel suede halter and the newly acquired cowboy boots that she had purchased the night before at Allen's Boot and Tack Shop near the ranch. Glancing in the mirror, she thought, *Boy, do I do Texas fabulous well!*

Alicia had changed quickly, but Valeria had still beaten her and was already in the kitchen waiting, wearing a pair of dusty jeans, a pink-pearl-buttoned cowboy shirt, and an honest-to-goodness white cowboy hat.

Valeria took in Alicia's ensemble. "You're not going to wear *that*, are you?"

"Why not?" Alicia said, grabbing a red apple from a big bowl on the wooden dining table. "I'm wearing jeans and a top, just like you."

Valeria took a deep breath, as though it were painful to hear the comparison. "How much did those jeans cost? Two hundred bucks?" she asked.

"Three," Alicia said, somewhat guiltily. "But they were a birthday present, and they are the only brand that fits me perfectly."

Valeria threw her hands up in the air. "*¡Ay, chica!* You

don't want to wear three-hundred-dollar jeans to go horseback riding! One, you're going to be really uncomfortable, and will probably get jean burn. Two, they are going to get filthy."

Alicia bristled. She was a practical girl. She ran her own company, for goodness' sake. What did Valeria take her for? She wasn't some coddled princess.

"I appreciate the advice, but I'll be fine," Alicia said dismissively. "One, these jeans are supercomfy. That's one of the reasons they were worth the price, and two, if they get dirty, I'll wash them. No *problema!*"

"Okay," Valeria said. "But your top is way too pretty for this ride. It's suede, and we're going to cross the shallow part of the river on this trip. The horses like to splash. And it's a halter—your back and arms are completely exposed to the sun, the bugs, and the brush. Please, I want this to be fun for you. Let me lend you some clothes."

Alicia stubbornly shook her head. "I'll just throw my cashmere cardi over the halter. Sorted."

There was no use arguing once Alicia made up her mind. Valeria had known her just long enough to have noticed that about her. Sighing, she let the matter drop and silently hoped Alicia wasn't going to regret her decision.

After grabbing her sweater, Alicia cheerfully followed Valeria out of the kitchen. She was excited to be having an authentic Texas experience. Sure, they were there to work. But eating open-pit barbecue in a town called Driftwood, riding on a horse across a river—this spring break was already shaping up to be one of the most memorable ones ever.

Valeria turned and glanced down at Alicia's feet. "Girl, I swear, I'm not trying to be annoying," she said sincerely, "but are those the boots we bought last night?"

Alicia nodded. "Cute, right?"

"Last piece of advice, I promise. But it takes a little while to break in a new pair of boots. We keep lots of extras at the stable. . . ." Valeria's voice trailed off when she saw Alicia's look. "You really want to wear those, huh?"

Alicia smiled and nodded, looking just like a little girl in a doll shop. "They are *so* cute. I can't take them off. They're like my Texas Cinderella slippers."

"Well, then, Cindy Ella, let's get to steppin'," Valeria said, giving up. "We want to be back and in the house before that noonday sun starts beating down."

The two girls walked along the rocky path from the guesthouse to the stables. Alicia was impressed with how well Valeria knew all the ranch workers; the night before, she had told them that the ranch employed forty-five people, half of whom lived on the grounds. When she was with the *amigas* and Gaz, Valeria seemed like a little bit of an awkward, albeit outspoken nerd— the stringy hair, the bad posture, the message T-shirts. But as she walked around the ranch, she seemed totally different.

"¿*Hola, Miguel, qué pasa?*" Valeria called out to a short guy baling hay. He waved enthusiastically.

"How's your beautiful little Elisabeta?" Valeria asked a woman grooming a dark brown horse.

As the daughter of Miami's deputy mayor and one of the city's most powerful judges, Alicia was used to navigating roomfuls of grown-ups. It was one of the things that made it so easy for her to deal with the parents of her *quince* clients. Valeria might have been in desperate need of a haircut and some lessons in teenage girl style, but out here on the ranch, she was confident in her own skin—and Alicia admired that.

"The stable houses more than two dozen horses," Valeria explained as they approached the big structure, "mostly, ranch horses that the staff and family ride. We used to have thoroughbreds. My father had hopes that I would ride competitively. But from the moment I took my first spin on a skateboard I've always been more excited about wheels than hooves. Don't get me wrong, I love horses and riding on the ranch, but it is never going to be my life."

"I get it," Alicia said. "I used to think that I would be a lawyer, like my mom was before she became a judge, or even run for office someday. I even had this crazy internship at the mayor's office last summer. It was fun, but then the *quince*-planning thing happened and I just knew that was what I wanted to do." She paused and then said, "We should figure out how to get 'boarding into your party."

Valeria nodded, looking animated at the idea. "If you want, I'll take you guys to the skateboard park where me and my friends like to hang," she said. "Ever been on a board before?"

Alicia shook her head. "I'm not so much the athletic type. Except for dance. I've been taking dance classes since I was a kid, and sometimes I think I'd love to be a choreographer. I like to think of planning a *quince* like choreographing an amazing ballet."

Valeria's eyes widened. "You like to dance?"

Alicia shrugged as though it were obvious. "Yeah, who doesn't? Everybody can dance. Not everybody can ride a horse or a skateboard."

"Not true," Valeria said softly. "I should have been

honest when I wrote you and told you that I'm not a great dancer. That was an understatement. I dance like a horse. Actually that would be an insult to those fine, graceful creatures. I'm worse than that. I never dance. Not in private. Not in public. I don't even tap my feet when I hear a song I like. That's how awful my sense of rhythm is."

"But you're going to dance at your own *quince*. *You've got to*," Alicia insisted.

Valeria didn't answer. Instead she led them into the barn's main aisle, where she then opened a stall door. She turned and looked at Alicia. "I'm a Castillo. We're a pretty proud breed. My *abuelo* was one of the first Texas cowboys. He came to Austin from Mexico without a penny when he was fourteen and found independent work as a *vaquero*, herding and helping to take care of other people's cattle. He had dreams of someday becoming a *ranchero*. Little by little, he began to acquire his own property. He's eighty-four now, and as you can see by everything that surrounds you, he figured out a way to make his dream come true. This is a man who came to Texas with nothing and ended up being the *patrón* of a thousand-acre ranch. We Castillos are fierce about following the beat of our own drum. It works for us. As far as I'm concerned, I don't *got* to do anything but stay true to my Chicana roots and get into a really good college."

Alicia laughed out loud. Valeria did have a weird sense of style and was offbeat and unassuming. But she was firm in her opinions, she spoke her mind, and she wasn't to be trifled with. Alicia was liking her more and more.

"Point taken," she said. "No dancing unless you want dancing. So, how about some riding?"

"Good idea," Valeria said, leading a white horse with brown spots out of the stall. "This is Maguire. She's the gentlest horse on the property. You'll ride her. She'll take good care of you."

Valeria clipped the cross-ties onto Maguire's halter so she couldn't go anywhere and then went to lead out a second horse out of his stall. He was a caramel-colored gelding with a shining white mane and tail.

"This is my baby, Greige," Valeria said.

"Oh, he's beautiful," Alicia said, running her fingers along the horse's silky side.

After a quick lesson in grooming and tacking up, it was time to ride. It took a few clumsy tries, but finally Alicia was able to pull herself up into the saddle. Then she sucked in her breath. It was higher up than it looked from the ground, and she feared she might topple over any second.

"Don't worry, we've had five-year-olds ride Maguire," Valeria said, trying to sound reassuring. "She won't let anything happen to you."

Valeria went over Riding 101 with Alicia. "You're going to use your legs to squeeze and your hands to give her signals," she said. "You can give her a light nudge with your foot if you want her to go faster. Give the rein a slight tug if you want her to stop. The main thing is to stay loose and relaxed."

Perched just a little stiffly on Maguire, Alicia followed Valeria past the cottages that housed the ranch staff and into a grove of cypress trees. As good a guide as any host on the Discovery Channel, Valeria named everything they saw.

"That's Indian paintbrush," she said, pointing to a dark red flower. "The Chippewa used it to make a shampoo that made their hair beautiful and glossy. They also made a medicine out of it. And those there are Texas bluebonnets."

"I have a question," Alicia said when they'd been riding for a while. Ever since arriving in Texas, something had been on her mind.

"Shoot," Valeria called back as her horse trotted a few feet ahead of Alicia's.

"Are *quinceañeras* not a big deal here?" Alicia asked. "'Cause, you—um, and don't get me wrong—but you sort of left it to the last minute, and in Miami, we usually plan from, like, the womb."

"Oh, they are," Valeria said. "This is Texas. Everyone loves a big party, especially one that involves good music, good food, and folks traveling in from all around."

Alicia, who was still slightly afraid that her horse might go tearing off in the opposite direction, asked shakily, "Then why leave yours for the very last minute?"

"Well, in my experience, the Castillo women are cursed with a *quince*-zilla gene," Valeria explained. "I'm trying really hard to avoid it."

Settling into a light trot, Alicia rode up next to her and said, "It happens to the best of us. I went all *quince*-zilla once, and it wasn't even my birthday."

"Trust me, you haven't seen a real *quince*-zilla until you see someone in my family. All of my cousins have turned their fifteenth birthday into some kind of crazy debutante-ball/*quinceañera*/let-me-show-you-how-much-money-my-family-has extravaganza.

"I want my *quince* to reflect my pride in my Latina roots, and I want to be honest about who I am," Valeria went on. "A slightly off-center, slightly goth, animal-loving, independent-thinking, Chicana skateboarder.

I want it to be traditional, but organic and loose—like riding a horse. And that's a tall order."

Alicia smiled. She loved a challenge. "Well, you called the right people," she said. "We'll come up with a *quince* that suits you perfectly."

CHAPTER 6

BY THE TIME Alicia arrived back at the ranch, all of the warm and fuzzy feelings from her ride and heart-to-heart with Valeria had faded. She was moaning in pain, a picture of misery. Her pretty clothes were covered in dirt, she was a pool of sweat, and her face, torso, and arms were all a bright beet red.

She was slumped in a La-Z-Boy in the great room, soaking her blistered feet in a bucket of cool water when the rest of her friends came back.

While the other girls went to shower, Gaz, ever the gentleman, who perhaps felt a teeny-tiny bit guilty that he had shirked his party-planning duties, sat down on the arm of the chair and began applying aloe to Alicia's burning limbs. "You know, Lici," he said gently, "sometimes it just doesn't pay to be so stubborn. If you had taken Valeria's advice, you wouldn't be looking and feeling like a fried tamale."

"Stop rubbing it in," groaned Alicia. Gaz stood up.

"No! I don't mean stop rubbing in the aloe! What I mean is, I don't need you to remind me that I acted like a know-it-all and an idiot. What I need you to do is to kiss me, before I start to cry."

Gaz leaned in. Minutes passed. Alicia forgot about the pain. Seemingly, they were trying for the world's longest lip-lock when Marisol and Ranya interrupted their marathon make-out session.

"Hey, Mom," a now even more red faced Alicia said, after she and Gaz pulled apart.

"Hey, Mrs. Cruz," Gaz said, looking down.

"Well, this is interesting," Marisol said. "How long have you been wearing Riviera Pink lipstick, Gaz?"

Startled, Gaz reached for a napkin and began to wipe his mouth.

"You missed a spot on your cheek," Marisol said as he turned a dark shade of crimson.

Ranya and Marisol looked at each other and burst out laughing.

"Ain't young love grand?" Ranya said. Then she got serious. "Gaz, I have some good news for you. I was able to pull some strings and get you tickets to a couple of panels for South by Southwest." She handed him a packet.

"You're kidding," he said, staring at the large manila envelope as though it would disappear at any moment.

"Not kidding," Ranya said. "I know a guy who knows a guy. Besides, I listened to your CD last night. Alicia gave it to me to review for Valeria's party. You're good. We want to show all of you the best that Texas has to offer. And maybe you can show those conference folks what Miami has to offer."

Gaz stood up and gave her a giant hug. "You probably changed my life today," he said solemnly.

"Well, remember me when you're famous," she replied, waving good-bye as she and Marisol left the room.

"Wow, that's pretty cool," Alicia said when they were gone. "Right?"

Gaz didn't answer. Instead, he ripped open the envelope, and then his mouth dropped open.

"Oh, my God, Lici," he said, quickly scanning the contents. "You should see the panels she's gotten me into: Building a High Value Fan List Online; The Ins and Outs of Indie Touring; Music Publishing: Making Money While You Sleep."

"Making Money While You Sleep," Alicia repeated. "That sounds good."

Gaz got to the last item in the packet and shook his

head. "Wait. This can't be right."

"What?" Alicia asked.

"It says here that she's got me a spot in the new-artist showcase. Hundreds of artists compete for each of the twenty-five three-minute slots. That showcase has been booked for over a year now."

"Well, whoever Ranya's friend is, they definitely know the right people," Alicia said.

"The first panel starts in three hours," Gaz said, getting up to call the ranch transportation crew. He stopped and looked back at his girlfriend. "Lici, are you okay with this? I know I need to get all the music together for Valeria's party, but this is a once-in-a-lifetime chance for me. But I promise you, I'll figure out a way to not fall down on the job."

"Promise?" asked Alicia.

"I promise," answered Gaz, giving her a hug and flashing an irresistible grin.

"Then *vaya con Dios, mi amor,*" Alicia purred.

"*Primero,*" he said, growing serious. "I just have to tell you thank you for being such an amazing girlfriend. You know how much my music means to me, and if it wasn't for you, this amazing opportunity would never have come my way."

"Well, you know, I try," Alicia said, kissing him again

softly on the lips. "But right now you've got to go make music history, and I've got a *quince* to plan."

Throughout the van ride into downtown Austin, Gaz clutched the envelope with his conference passes so tightly that his knuckles were white. Despite the fact that it was a perfect spring day—balmy, breezy, and not too hot—he kept his window firmly shut, lest the envelope fly out of his hands right out the window, and with it all the dreams he had for his career.

Luis, the driver, tried to engage him in conversation, asking him questions about Miami, the weather in Florida, gator sightings. But Gaz was too nervous to talk, and eventually Luis gave up. Gaz kept thinking about his late father. Felipe Colón had been a musician in Puerto Rico before he passed away from cancer. When he was a kid, Gaz loved to hear his father play at the small concert halls in San Juan. His music made people laugh with joy, dance in the streets, sing along, and sometimes even cry. Gaz hoped to be able to do the same thing one day.

Finally, they arrived at the conference. Luis made his way through the crazy traffic and dropped Gaz off at the conference registration hall. "Hey, man," Gaz said speaking for the first time. "Thanks for the ride. Sorry to be so distracted. I just have this feeling that everything I do or say today has the potential to make or break my career."

Luis smiled. "I get it. South by Southwest. It's a big deal. But try to relax; enjoy yourself. Let some of the good stuff come to you, or you'll find yourself always chasing the next big thing. *Adiós, chico,* and *buena suerte.*"

Luis drove off. For a moment, Gaz didn't move. He just stood in front of the building, wishing his father were still alive to see him play, to see that even at sixteen, Gaz was taking the music seriously.

Finally, he walked inside and over to the registration desk. After checking in, he hung his laminated credentials card around his neck and began to explore.

His first panel of the day was called Songwriting 101 and featured names that the ordinary music public would never know—Edith Norell, Susanna Toobin, Shawn Brinks, and Hiro Utada. Even though their names weren't well known, among them, the four songwriters had written sixteen number-one songs and won two dozen Grammys. Gaz remembered fondly how he and his brothers had played Shawn Brinks's "Bump This. Jump This. Thump This" at their very first school talent show, in the sixth grade. They had been kind of pathetic, but also had been so excited to be up on a stage that it hadn't even bothered them.

Finding his way to the designated room, he took a seat in the back. While the panel members spoke, he took notes more fervently than he ever had at any class in school. At the end, when the moderator, Kenneth Sanchez, a popular Austin radio DJ, called for questions, Gaz willed his hand to rise, but couldn't find the courage.

However, when Kenneth called, "Last question!" not only did Gaz's hand shoot in the air, but his whole body went with it.

Kenneth laughed, and the whole room joined him. "The last question goes to Mr. Enthusiasm, sitting in the last row," the DJ said.

Gaz stood up. He cleared his throat nervously. "All of you have written songs that have touched literally millions of people. But to hear you talk today, each and every one of your songs is incredibly personal. How do you make your personal feelings matter to the world?" He was surprised to hear his voice sounding deep and confident when he spoke, even though he felt nervous inside.

"Good question," Kenneth said. "Who wants to answer?"

Susanna Toobin lifted her microphone. "I'll take this one." She was a petite woman with long dark hair and blunt-cut bangs. Even though she hadn't played a note, she sat cross-legged with a guitar on her lap, as if the inspiration to jam might hit at any time. "What's your name?" she asked.

"Gaspar," he told her.

She smiled. "Well, Gaspar, I love your question. As I mentioned before, I'm from Chicago, and for me one of the touchstones of my writing life is the great Chi-town playwright Lorraine Hansberry, who said—and I'm paraphrasing—'to achieve the universal you must pay incredible attention to the specific.' That's the way to make the personal reach out and touch others. At least, I hope it is, or else I'm going to go out of business real fast."

The room was filled with chuckles. "Thank you," Gaz said, softly, flushing because he was aware that so many of the eyes in the room were still on him.

The moderator stood. "I think that's a great note to end on," he announced. "Please give our panelists a round of applause."

Gaz clapped loudly, and when the room was nearly empty, he finally picked up his backpack to leave. He was outside the seminar room fumbling for his schedule when a girl approached him.

"Hi," she said. "I'm Saniyah. And you're Gaspar, right? What kind of name is that?"

"It's complicated," he said, blushing.

Saniyah tilted her head and smiled. "I can handle 'complicated.'"

Gaz shifted his weight from one foot to the other, unsure of what to say next. The girl *seemed* to be flirting, and he wasn't used to flirting—unless it was with Alicia. Saniyah was not especially tall, but with boots on she could nearly look Gaz directly in the eyes. She had olive skin, dark curly hair, and her lips were stained a shade of burgundy that made Gaz think of red wine and old-fashioned movie stars.

"Good job in there," she went on when he didn't flirt back—or speak. "Your question really made an impression on Susanna Toobin and Kenneth Sanchez. I heard them talking about how it was one of the most insightful questions either of them had been asked since this conference began."

Gaz didn't know what to say. How could such a thing be possible? He felt as though he were back in elementary school, when the kids would declare it Opposite Day. Girls who couldn't stand you would tell you that they loved you. Guys who normally shunned you during gym invited you first to play on their team. You'd be feeling pretty good about yourself, and then they'd scream, "Opposite Day!" and everything would come crashing back down to crappy normal.

Gaz couldn't let himself believe it. "Really?" he finally said.

"Really. They clearly thought you were the smartest guy in the room," Saniyah said. "And you know, this business is all about relationships. You did give Susanna Toobin your business card before she left, right?"

"Business card?" Gaz repeated.

"Uh, duh. Please don't tell me you came to South by Southwest without any business cards," she said, as if the thought of it caused her real physical pain. "This is more than an industry conference, it's a celestial event! The biggest names in media, music, film, and technology are all *here*, and you don't have business cards?"

Gaz fished around in his wallet. "I don't have any for my music, but I do have this." He pulled out a card. Saniyah scanned it quickly.

AMIGAS INCORPORATED
GAZ COLÓN
DJ and Live Music
Because your *quinceañera* is much more than a party

"*Amigas* Incorporated," Saniyah read, emphasizing the word *amigas*. "You are a man, aren't you?"

Gaz felt a familiar rush of annoyance. "I didn't choose the name. It's a *quinceañera* business I have in Miami with my friends." Gaz knew that this would have been the perfect moment to bring up Alicia. All he had to say was, *It's a business I have with my* girl-friend *and her friends.* But he was in a new city, at an amazing music conference, talking to an admittedly very pretty girl. He didn't want to just be Gaz from Miami, who lived with his mother in a rich family's guesthouse so he could be eligible to attend the elite public school nearby. He didn't want to be Gaz, who worked double shifts at the Gap to help his family out and played *quince* gigs on the side to bring in extra cash. He wanted to be something more, something new, and being in Austin gave him the clean-slate feeling that he craved. He could tell Saniyah about Lici later.

Saniyah handed the Amigas Inc. card back to him. "This isn't going to cut it here at South by Southwest. Lucky for you, I have a friend who works at a local copy place. He can whip you up a hundred business cards in an hour."

She took out her cell phone and started dialing. Then she rattled off Gaz's name, his cell phone number, and all the relevant details. Before she hung up, she said, "Thanks for this, Toby. I owe you one."

Turning back to Gaz, she said, "Business cards are in the hopper. Let's talk sched. Where are you playing this week, Gaspar?"

Saniyah was like a tornado. She just had swept in and was changing everything. Actually, Gaz thought, she was more like a fairy godmother—a really cute, funny, and young one. And he liked the way she used his full name. She made it sound so much better than his mother did when she was mad at him and screamed, "Gaspar Roberto Orlando Colón, clean up your room!"

"I've got a slot in the new-artist showcase," he said proudly.

"Impressive. I couldn't get in, and I've been working the conference angle for months." Saniyah sighed. "But where else are you playing? You've got to try to get a gig locally. Restaurants. Barbecue joints. Open-mike nights. All the talent execs in town are going to be out eating and drinking. You've got to book some casual walk-in spots. Give somebody famous an opportunity to discover you."

Gaz's head was spinning. There was so much to take in and so much he was clueless about. He had thought the panels would be enough, but obviously there was way more to the conference. "Wow," he said, sighing. "I had no idea how little I knew. Thanks for looping me in. How can I pay you back?"

Saniyah smiled. "Well, you can start by taking me to a late lunch. I'm starving."

CHAPTER 7

THAT NIGHT, the Castillo family invited the Miami gang out to the Hacienda Cafe in San Marcos, one of the family's favorite Hill Country spots.

In the van on the way over, Valeria was quiet until Carmen asked her about their destination. At that, she perked up. "The Hill Country is famous for its rolling hills and miles and miles of wildflowers. Its been recognized by several of the world's leading magazines as one of the ten best places 'to live the simple life.' And to top it all off, Willie Nelson sometimes hangs out there. How cool is that?"

"How do you know all these things?" asked Alicia when Valeria paused to take a breath.

"My daughter is a bit of a Texas history buff," answered David. "If there's anything you want to know about the Lone Star State, she's your go-to girl."

Valeria blushed. "My dad's exaggerating, of course,

but what I do know about Texas is that the Hacienda has great eats and even greater line dancing. Their house band is one of the best Tejano groups in the city. I really think you're going to like it."

Alicia grinned. "Sounds awesome. But I thought you hated dancing."

Valeria shrugged. "I hate to dance, but I love music, and I love to watch people dance. I just know my limits," she explained. "Speaking of which, while I loved our ride this morning, I'm sorry you're so sore."

"Sore" was an understatement. Alicia was sitting with an ice pack on each thigh. "I wouldn't blame you if you played the I-Told-You-So card," she replied.

"I'd be happy to say it for her," Jamie teased. Then she asked Valeria, "Speaking of which, how *was* our cowgirl in the saddle?"

"It was just a short ride, and, given the time she had to get used to being back up on a horse, she did pretty well."

Alicia emphatically shook her head. "You guys have seen how she is at measuring distances! It was a two-hour ride, at least. I could qualify for the Olympics with the amount of time I spent in that saddle."

Valeria leaned back to whisper to Carmen, "Is she always this dramatic?"

"Oh, yes," Carmen replied. "Our Lici is quite the actress."

"Hello, sitting right here!" Alicia protested, trying to shift her sore body into a more comfortable position.

"Valeria did tell you not to wear those skintight fancy jeans while you were horseback riding," Jamie reminded her friend.

"Hey, not fair," Alicia muttered. "They're not skintight. They're my cowboy jeans."

"Speaking of cowboys, where's Gaz?" Carmen asked.

Alicia shifted the ice pack. "Since the restaurant is pretty close to the conference center, he's going to meet us there."

"Well, you won't have to wait much longer," Valeria said. "We're here."

The group—except for Alicia, who was a bit slower and took her time—all scrambled out of the van and headed toward the rather unassuming building with the flashing sign that read: BBQ*BEER*RIBS. HOME OF THE HOT STUFF!

Jamie was the first to get to the restaurant doors. When she opened them, she let out a long, low whistle.

Alicia, who had finally gotten out of the van, looked over. "Is it that bad?" she asked, assuming Jamie's reaction was to the decor.

But the decor had nothing to do with it. Jamie had been stopped in her tracks by the people. One person in particular. "Just wondering . . . who is *she*?"

Alicia followed her friend's gaze and suddenly understood her reaction. The Castillo family had booked the Hacienda Cafe's largest table—a long wooden table on a raised platform, covered with a canopy of twinkling lights. And, at one end, Gaz sat, laughing and talking . . . with a girl whom none of them recognized.

He rose as they approached. "Hi, Valeria, I hope it's okay if I brought someone. I called your mother and asked for permission, and she said it was fine with her. Saniyah has been such a huge help to me at the conference, I invited her to have dinner with us."

"Okay by me," said Valeria. "Nice to meet you, Saniyah."

If Alicia hadn't been suffering from a severe sunburn, the sight of Gaz huddled at a table chatting away with some unknown hottie would have made her deathly pale. Summoning up all her self-control, she put on her best game face and went over to greet Saniyah. Alicia was dressed in her best version of southwestern chic— a strapless denim dress, a red bandanna headband, and her red sandals. Unfortunately, that didn't help the fact that her riding injuries made her hobble over to the table in what could only be called a sad impersonation of Hopalong Cassidy. She straightened and held out a hand. "I'm Alicia," she said, smiling as she added, "Gaz's girlfriend."

It was clear from the tight expression on Saniyah's face that Gaz had neglected to mention having a girlfriend. Carmen and Jamie exchanged nervous glances.

Unaware of the drama brewing, Valeria's parents and Alicia's mom made themselves comfortable at the opposite end of the table from Gaz. Valeria and Jamie took seats on either side of Saniyah. And Carmen, in hopes of being a stabilizing influence, sat between Alicia and Gaz.

To Alicia's annoyance, after her first reaction, Saniyah didn't seem to give much thought to Gaz's relationship status. "Well, it's really nice to meet all of Gaspar's friends," she said, once everyone was seated.

Alicia smiled thinly. "How interesting. It seems you and Gaz have become close. Yet, we know absolutely nothing about you. Enlighten us."

Before Saniyah could answer, the DJ started playing a song, and she jumped up. "Do you guys know this song? It's a classic. 'That's How We Country Boys Roll.' Gaspar, wanna dance?"

Gaz shrugged but found himself being dragged

onto the dance floor. Alicia stayed where she was—for all of five seconds. There was no way she was letting her man dance with another girl. She got up and started to hobble after them.

"Hey, Alicia," Carmen called, "if you're still hurting from your horseback ride, no shame in sitting this one out."

Alicia turned and glared at her. "I *never* sit a dance out. Dancing is my thing."

Valeria had been up talking to her mother. Now she walked over and put a hand on her shoulder. "*Chica*, I saw the blisters you're sporting, and I think at the moment, sitting might be your thing."

Alicia looked over to where Saniyah was teaching Gaz a basic Texas line dance. "Oh, my God, it's like a country-and-western Macarena." She rolled her eyes. "I can do a Macarena with my eyes closed, doesn't matter how sore my feet and butt are."

Valeria tried to warn her. "It's actually a little more complicated than it seems. . . ." But Alicia just ignored her.

Carmen shook her head. "It's no use trying to talk sense into her."

"Once Lici's made up her mind, there's no stopping her," Jamie said. "Might as well join her, give her moral support. She's going to need it."

Back in Miami, discussing their trip, the group had agreed that line dancing had high cornball potential. Saniyah, however, made it look graceful. Therefore, they were unprepared for just how hard it was. They all tried to keep up as she tapped her heels and sashayed this way and that, but the most they could catch was a hip swivel here and a hop there. Still, they were having fun. The group danced their way through Josh Turner, Billy Currington, Alan Jackson, Carrie Underwood, and Tim McGraw.

One by one, though, they each dropped out. Valeria was hungry and wanted to order food. Carmen wanted to text Domingo before dinner started, which reminded Jamie that she wanted to call Dash. Gaz, who had never really gotten the hang of the moves, bowed out, too. Soon, it was a very uneven dance-off between Saniyah and Alicia, who was scooting around like a grandmother on her way to Tuesday-night bingo.

Saniyah looked as though she could have danced all night.

"We call this one the Wild Wild West," she explained as she began a new step.

"That looks a lot like a merengue to me," Alicia snapped, trying to add some Latin flavor to it. But she succeeded only in causing herself pain, as her shirt chafed against her sunburned skin.

Carmen and Jamie, having contacted their sweeties, came back and stood on the sidelines cheering their best *amiga* on. "Go, Lici, go, Lici," they cried as their friend gave every move her best shot. They exchanged looks when she got distracted. They hated to admit it, but if this had been an official dance contest, Saniyah would have been cruising to first place.

On the next song, Saniyah changed things up again. "This one is so old-school! It's called the Cowboy Charleston."

Alicia had welts on her feet, her inner thighs were saddle sore, and her sunburned face, arms, and legs ached even more intensely. All she wanted to do was lie down in a cool bath, then take a three-day nap. But she was beginning to feel as though this were the finale on *Dancing with the Stars*. She'd come too far to quit. Out of sheer desperation, she began to do the dance that required the least amount of movement—the Robot— which drew a huge whoop from the small crowd that had gathered to watch her and Saniyah work it out on the dance floor.

When the song ended, Alicia was sure there would be no more. That she could finally sit down. But then

Billy Ray Cyrus's "Achy Breaky Heart" came on, and the crowd roared. Alicia seriously considered getting down on the floor and doing an old hip-hop move called the Worm. She figured she could scooch across the floor to the rhythm, and, if nothing else, she'd win points for originality. But just as she got to her knees, she heard her joints crack and she realized that if she got down, she might not be able to get up.

"Help," she said in the tiniest of voices. Carmen and Jamie rushed to her side and helped her over to the table.

"You okay there, Achy-Breaky?" Jamie asked when they were safely seated.

"If I ever go on *Survivor*, I'm taking you," Carmen said. "You are a girl who doesn't know the meaning of the word *quit*."

Alicia groaned. Looking at the dance floor, where her rival continued to sway, she wished that that were true. But sometimes, even the best of boots were meant for sitting.

A while later, a waiter sporting a felt ten-gallon hat with the words BOSS OF THE PLAINS cross-stitched across the brim, arrived with baskets of warm bread and dipping sauce.

Alicia reached for a piece of jalapeño corn bread

as Valeria started to say, "One thing about the corn bread . . ."

Too late. Alicia had popped it in her mouth and started chewing. Her face immediately turned bright red. She downed a glass of water, then knocked back Carmen's, too.

"First my legs were on fire, now it's my mouth. Ohhhh," she moaned, fanning her face.

"I was trying to tell you, the corn bread is really spicy," Valeria said.

"Are you okay?" Saniyah asked sweetly, sounding as though she meant it—sort of.

"Fine!" Alicia said, straightening up in her chair. "Just fine. But enough about me. What about *you*? What's your life story? How'd you meet my Gaz?"

"Not much to tell," Saniyah said, avoiding taking the bait. "My mother is Persian and grew up in Mexico City. My dad is from Costa Rica, and he went to med school at the University of Mexico. He's in public health. My mom teaches in the classics department at UT Austin. And I'm a Texas girl, born to sing and play guitar. Just like Gaspar, music is the most important thing in my life. That's why I've promised to show him the ropes while he's here in Austin."

"Fascinating," Alicia said, studying the menu and

looking anything but fascinated. She clenched her teeth. "It's so generous of you to take him under your wing."

"How about you guys?" Saniyah asked, not letting Alicia's attitude get to her. "You're from Miami, right? Gaspar said you're here to plan Valeria's *quince*. How cool is that?"

Valeria smiled shyly. "I'm really grateful to have them here."

The tension was still high when the waiter came by to take their order. Up on the stage, the house band, Agua Caliente, was getting ready. To distract everyone from the awkward dynamic at the table while they waited for their food, Jamie started babbling away about the customization details of each sneaker in her collection while everyone except an enraptured Valeria, listened to her with eyes glazing over.

Twenty of the longest minutes ground slowly past. Finally, the waiter returned, with trays of food. "*Buen provecho*, amigos," he remarked as he placed several platters filled with steaming Tex-Mex food on the long wooden table.

Smiling, Saniyah asked, "Do you have anything with more heat than the house hot sauce?"

He nodded. "One bottle of Ring of Fire coming right up."

Seconds later, he returned and handed the bottle to Saniyah, who doused her entire plate of ribs and smashed potatoes with it.

"Wow," Gaz said, looking impressed. "I tasted the sauce on the table and it was hot. Do you have a four-octave voice to match your four-octave pepper range?"

Saniyah looked down as though embarrassed. "You know what they say about the heat and the kitchen." Then she began to sing an old blues song, in the loveliest light soprano voice any of them had ever heard.

Not to be outdone, and more than happy to cut off Saniyah's little sing-along, Alicia signaled for the waiter. "Um, excuse me," she said. "That Ring of Fire sauce is pretty bland."

"But you didn't even try it," Valeria pointed out.

Ignoring her, Alicia asked the waiter, "What do you have that's hotter?"

He looked at her dubiously. "Next up in terms of heat is Crazy Mother Pucker's Maniacal Mustard."

Carmen put a hand on her friend's arm. "Lici, don't do this."

Jamie, resorting to more desperate measures, kicked Alicia under the table, earning a glare. Alicia, it would seem, was not to be swayed.

When the waiter returned with the sauce, Valeria

suggested, "Maybe you should try a few drops, just to taste it."

Stuck in stubborn gear, Alicia shook her head. "I'm sure it will be wonderful." She doused her plate with the sauce, cut a piece of chicken, and put it in her mouth. There were exactly three seconds of silence before she began to choke so hard that not even sips of water could help.

"We'll be right back," she whispered, dragging Carmen with her to the bathroom.

Once the two girls were safely ensconced in the restroom, Alicia began waving her hands in front of her face. "My mouth is on fire," she lisped. "My tongue is swollen. Everything hurts. Please! Stop the burning."

"Give me a second," Carmen said, doing her best not to add, *you idiot.* She left and returned a few moments later with a cup of milk, two slices of white bread, and Alicia's mom.

"Why is my mom here?" Alicia sputtered between gulps of the milk.

"Because you're a hot Texas mess right now," Carmen said. "I had to call in serious backup."

Mrs. Cruz sat down on the sink next to her daughter. "You know, you're not the first girl to be jealous over her boyfriend's female friends," she said softly. "It's a tough lesson, but one you might as well learn now. It's never about the other girl. Just like, if the tables were turned and you met a boy who shared a common interest, it wouldn't be about Gaz. You've got to trust the people you love and wish for them as broad and wide a circle of friends as you'd want for yourself."

Alicia stuck out her lower lip. "Gaz's circle of friends is wide enough. I don't want it to be any wider."

Her mother gave her a kiss on the forehead. "Maybe not at this exact moment, but someday, you will. How about I take you home?"

"Sounds good," Alicia said.

Turning to Carmen, Marisol said, "Can you make our excuses?"

"Of course." Then, hugging her best friend, Carmen said, "See you in a little bit."

Although she was usually the last to concede defeat, Alicia had to admit it felt good to get into the van with her mother and rest her head on her lap. And while, in classic Texas-speak, Valeria would've insisted that the restaurant was "right down the street," it was actually nearly an hour's drive back to the ranch. By the time Luis pulled up to the front door of the Castillo family guesthouse, Alicia was sound asleep. And, for the moment, her troubles were forgotten.

CHAPTER 8

THE NEXT MORNING, Alicia woke to a soft knock on the door. It was Gaz, holding two thermoses.

Chagrined by the memory of her hot-sauce bravado, she hadn't bothered to try to stay up till he got home the night before. She hadn't wanted to discuss with either Gaz or her *amigas* the four-alarm jealousy she had felt when she met Saniyah and saw how much the girl and Gaz had in common.

"Get dressed and then meet me downstairs," he whispered, peeping his head through the door. "Let's go for a walk."

And because she was more embarrassed now than angry, she knew the best and only thing to do was to agree.

It was cooler in Texas than Alicia, used to the humid Miami weather, could've imagined. Even though it was the spring season, it was certifiably chilly at times—especially during the early mornings and the evenings, after the sun had set.

She quickly brushed her teeth, threw her hair into a messy bun, and put on a thick, soft merino turtleneck over her T-shirt and pajama pants. She stole a peek at the grandfather clock. Six thirty a.m. By all appearances, everyone in the house was still sleeping.

She found Gaz sitting on the top step of the guesthouse porch. He was lost in thought and for a moment, Alicia just took in his handsome features. Then she made a noise and he looked up. Smiling, he signaled to her that they should be quiet, and they put on their coats and boots in silence.

"Gaz, where are we going?" Alicia asked in a whisper once they were outside.

"Follow me," he said confidently. He led the way down a winding dirt path toward the working part of the ranch. In his hand he held a giant flashlight, although why that was, Alicia didn't really know. Dawn was breaking, and they could see well enough not to get lost.

"Gaz," she began, as the path curved around a field of sleeping cows. "I'm sorry about last night. I . . ."

"Wait," Gaz interrupted. "We're almost there."

The sky was getting lighter, and shadows were giving way to scenes of stirring life. Just ahead, she could make out the red and white henhouse. Was that where they were going? she wondered. To get fresh eggs for the *migas*?

But they continued on. They passed a parked John Deere tractor, and finally they stopped. Gaz took a seat on a bench near one of the smaller corrals. "We're here," he said, triumphantly.

Alicia cocked her head. "Here" didn't seem all that exciting. Still, she wasn't one to throw stones. Not after last night. She took a seat on the bench next to him and opened up her thermos. The drink inside was hot and chocolaty.

"What is this?" Alicia asked after tasting the sweet drink.

"Nilka, the Castillo's cook, called it Aztec chocolate," Gaz said.

"It's so good," Alicia said, leaning against him and feeling blissfully calm.

For a moment there was nothing but the soft sounds of their sipping and the chirps of the early birds hunting the worms.

Then they both spoke at once. "I'm sorry—" They laughed awkwardly, and Gaz went on. "I'm sorry I didn't tell Saniyah that I had a girlfriend. I've been trying to figure out why, and I think it's just that I felt so out of my element at the conference. Everyone is so professional, so on top of their game. Saniyah is a sophomore, just like us. But she's already got a regular gig at a local coffeehouse. She's written a hundred songs and is trying to shop for a publishing deal with a major label."

Alicia tried to rein in her jealousy as he gushed about the other girl. Her mom's words echoed in her head.

Gaz took her hand, his expression serious. "Lici, before yesterday, I didn't even know what a music publishing deal was—or how to get major artists to hear my songs. You helped me get to the conference, and now Saniyah's helping me to take advantage of it. I'm grateful to you both. Coming here is the most important thing I've ever done for my career. I think I downplayed us because I didn't want it to seem that I landed in Austin just for some girl's *quince*, even though both you and I know that's the truth. I wanted to pretend, for at least a little while, that I had the focus and the drive—and the talent—to get here on my own."

Alicia squeezed Gaz's hand and leaned over to kiss him gently on the lips. She knew the feeling he was describing, the desire to make it on one's own. It was the same feeling that had pushed her to form Amigas Inc.

It was what pushed her every time they sat down with a new client and she vowed to give each girl the best Sweet Fifteen she'd ever seen. She couldn't fault Gaz for feeling the same way, even if it made her feel left out.

"You may not have come here on your own," Alicia said, "but you've got what it takes to make it, Gaz. And I'm glad Saniyah is helping you out."

The last part wasn't entirely true, but the sentiment behind it was. Alicia wanted Gaz to succeed, and if that meant others had to help him, well, she'd suck it up. As much as she could.

"And I owe you an apology, too. I'm sorry for acting like such a jerk last night," she went on. "Please forgive me?"

"I was never even mad at you. Not really," Gaz said, smiling and sending shivers through her. "So we're good." Then, as if to seal the deal, he kissed her with lips that tasted of chocolate and cinnamon.

She nodded. "We're definitely good."

While they were talking, the sun had risen over the horizon. Gaz looked at his watch. It was 6:58. "It's just about time for the show."

"What show?" Alicia asked.

Gaz looked to his left toward the stream and indicated that she should do the same. "Wait for it. . . .

Wait for it. . . . Here it comes."

Alicia let out a small shriek as half a dozen black and white antelopes charged by her, dashing across the field before disappearing into the hills. They were bigger than she would've imagined—like small ponies—and their coats were shiny and glossy, as if they'd also discovered the formula for Indian paintbrush shampoo. She took it all in—the wild majesty of the antelopes racing, the warm colors of the rising sun—and then, way too soon, it was over.

"That was awesome!" Alicia said, hugging Gaz. "How did you know? We just got here. How could you possibly know where to sit, what time they would come?"

Gaz smiled. "Luis told me. I sat next to him on the ride home last night, and I asked him if there was a good place for us to take a morning walk. He told me about the antelopes. They're actually blesboks, a rare African antelope that's somehow become part of the Texas Hill Country landscape. They belong to the neighboring ranch, but they like to come to the Castillo stream for their early-morning drink. Luis said that watching them with a special person is the best way to start the day."

Alicia smiled and squeezed his hand. "I think he's right."

CHAPTER 9

ARM IN ARM, Gaz and Alicia returned to the guesthouse. After a breakfast of huevos rancheros, topped off with home-grown salsa made from fresh tomatoes and jalapeño peppers picked right out of the Castillo family garden, Gaz went back to the conference to attend a panel on composing music for mobile applications, while Alicia took a shower and got dressed. It was time—no, it was *past* time—to get down to serious business.

After Gaz left, the remaining members of Amigas Inc. had a strategy meeting and then, around lunchtime, walked the short path to the Castillo family house to meet with their *quince* and hammer out details. On the way to dinner the night before, Valeria had mentioned wanting to show them something that would give them a sense of what she wanted for her party. They were curious to see what was in store.

Inside, the group congregated in what Valeria called the great room—a giant space that seemed part living room, part ballroom, and part family room, with thirty-foot ceilings and a giant stone fireplace.

Four giant sofas—each could easily have fit three Texas linebackers *and* their coach—made a square around an oversize wooden coffee table. The low table was covered with plates already set for lunch—guacamole with serrano chilis, freshly made tortillas, manchego cheese with figs, and a pitcher of cactus lemonade.

Jamie lay down across the couch nearest the fireplace. "This is what I'm talking about. Wake me when it's time to go back to Miami."

Carmen took a seat next to Valeria, whose long, unruly hair looked as if it hadn't seen a brush in days. The *quince*-to-be was wearing a black T-shirt that said, BARBIE WAS A VAMPIRE, and displayed a picture of a doll sporting fangs.

"Cool T-shirt," Alicia said, plopping cross-legged on the floor in a position strategically located between the guacamole and the chips.

Valeria smiled. But they could tell she was a little nervous. She pulled her laptop out of her bag and said, "So, like I said, I have something I wanted to show you.

It's a PowerPoint presentation I made for my mother when we first started discussing this female ritual. I support the tradition and the ceremony one hundred percent, but it's the big party element about which I remain deeply ambivalent."

Jamie sat up and clapped her hands. "So, we're going antiestablishment *quinceañera*? I love it!"

Alicia looked skeptical. "Um, great. You know, we're kind of antiestablishment, too."

"Not really," Carmen muttered, "but please, let's roll the tape."

Valeria hit a button, and the slide show began. The first image was a picture of her, wearing a fake mustache and poufy pink dress and holding a sign that said: ALWAYS A *DAMA*, NEVER A *QUINCE*.

Valeria hit the button again. "Exhibit A, my cousin Laura." In the picture, the *quince* was heavily made up, with Rapunzel hair down to her waist. She was wearing a white dress with exaggerated raglan sleeves, elbow-length gloves, and a giant rhinestone necklace.

"Her hair is so long," Carmen said. "Are those—"

"Yep," Valeria said. "Extensions."

The next picture was of Laura and her court, all wearing shiny silver dresses that looked as though they were made of aluminum foil. Valeria was front and center among the *damas,* a tortured grin substituting for a smile.

"OMG," Carmen said. "Her dress is bad, but those *dama* dresses are hideous."

"It's like something out of a sci-fi film. An alien *quince,*" Alicia said, shivering slightly.

Jamie stood and did a robot dance, saying, "I have come from the planet of the worse *quince* ever. Please meet our leader, Laura."

Valeria hit the button yet again. "Exhibit B, my cousin Loretta." In what was clearly a Western-themed *quince,* Loretta wore a big white cowboy hat, a short strapless dress with an abundance of fringe, and white cowboy boots.

"Are those buttons on her dress?" Carmen asked, peering closer.

"Nope, them be studs," Valeria said, putting heavy emphasis on her Texan twang. "'Cause Loretta's totally boy crazy and has always been interested in collecting studs. Get it?"

The other girls groaned.

"Oh, but there's more," said Valeria. She pulled up the next picture. All the *damas* wore white tube tops and prairie skirts emblazoned with the Texas state flag. And standing in the middle of her court, showing the camera her booty, Loretta let the world know that her panties had a Texas flag on them, too.

Carmen stifled a laugh. "Well, she's nothing if not patriotic."

"No need to be so polite," Valeria said, shaking her head. "She couldn't help it. She was really drunk. As part of the theme, the fruit punch was served in big ceramic jugs that said, 'moonshine.' Some of the losers from Loretta's school thought it might be funny to spike the punch, so it actually was as potent as moonshine. My poor cousin has trouble toning it down under the best of circumstances. You saw her dress. She chose it when she was sober. But she didn't stand a chance once she got a couple of drinks in her." She looked back at the keyboard, finger poised. "I have plenty more to show you. My dad has three sisters, and my mom has five brothers, so there are lots of *quince* pictures to share."

Alicia put the lid of the laptop down. "I think we've seen enough."

"We get it," Carmen said. "You're *quince*-party-averse."

"That's putting it mildly," Valeria said with a sigh. "My cousins turned their *quinces* into total spectacles. They didn't even seem to care about the tradition that makes the whole event so amazing."

"But the *quinces* we plan are *cool*," Jamie pointed out. "And they are all about the girl, not some demented attempt to impress people."

Alicia scooped some guacamole onto a chip, her expression thoughtful. "I have an idea," she finally said. "Why don't we do some serious damage to this guac while you go upstairs and bring back three items that represent your style?"

Valeria looked dubious. "Do you mean clothing? Because I'm not that into clothes."

Alicia shook her head. "I wasn't being literal. It doesn't have to be clothing. It could be music, a photo, a piece of jewelry. Whatever."

About twenty minutes later, the guacamole was finished and a beaming Valeria had returned. "That was fun!" she said. "But I couldn't choose just three items. So I brought down five."

"Bring it on," Alicia said.

"The first item is my skateboard; I couldn't live without it," Valeria said. "If you guys weren't here, I'd be at the skate park right now."

Alicia scribbled something in her notebook. "Skateboard. Okay, next."

"This is my birthday gift from my parents last year," Valeria said. "A black iPod. Limited edition, with an

Emily the Strange pic on the back. She's my favorite character and graphic-design icon. An artist, a skateboarder, and a race-car driver came up with her, and they started a company called Cosmic Debris. All of their products feature Emily's image and her famous sayings, like 'Get Lost,' 'Be All You Can't Be,' and 'Wish You Weren't Here.' My room is full of her stuff."

"I like this," Carmen said, assessing the iPod. "She's got a cool style. Classic black shift. Dark red lips. Love the bangs."

"The third item is the T-shirt I'm wearing," Valeria said. "Barbie Was a Vampire is my favorite band. I really believe in feminist goth music with a global consciousness."

"That's going to be a challenge for Gaz," Jamie cracked.

"We'll make it work," Alicia said. "You are rocking this assignment, Valeria. We might have to make this an official *quince* quiz for all our clients. What's next?"

"This is a photo of my mom on her wedding day," Valeria said. The girls all oohed and aahed. "That's a traditional Mexican dress. Doesn't she look beautiful? She bought it for fifteen dollars at a roadside store in Laredo. She and my father were graduate students on vacation in Baja. They had absolutely no loot. When my father saw my mother in this dress, he proposed. They eloped and got married on the beach the next day."

The girls were uncharacteristically silent, each lost in thought, transported to a Baja beach and a romantic wedding.

"Wow, that's an incredible story," Alicia finally said softly.

"I want a love story like that," Jamie added.

"You and Dash already have one. Girl defies country-club tradition, amazing athlete falls head over heels in love with her. Your story is pretty good, *chica*," Carmen said.

"But Valeria's parents eloping. It's like something straight out of a movie," Jamie said.

"It is *so-o-o* like a movie," Alicia agreed.

"I know. That's why this picture makes me happy," Valeria said. "They still look at each other in exactly this way."

Alicia picked up her notebook. "I hate to move on, but the clock is ticking. What's next?"

Valeria handed her a big old-fashioned silver key. "Big" was an understatement. It looked like something from *Alice in Wonderland* and was the size of Valeria's laptop.

Alicia laughed. "I know everything is bigger in Texas, but what the heck is this?"

Valeria nodded. "It's the original key to the ranch gates. My father gave it to me when I got into my high school, the Ann Richards School for Young Women Leaders. He wanted me to always remember that there was no door that was ever truly closed; it's always a matter of finding the right key."

"I'm going to cry," Carmen said softly.

"Me, too," Jamie said.

"Okay," Alicia teased. "You've made us all weepy, V. We need to get up and have an Amigas group hug."

"I'm not a really big hugger," said Valeria. "But with you guys, I'm willing to give it a try." Standing up slowly, she edged forward and joined the others in an embrace.

"So, what do we think, *chicas*?" Alicia asked when they pulled apart. "Where do we go from here?"

"Please don't be offended," Carmen said, taking Valeria by the hand. "But I think we need to start with a makeover. You are one of the smartest, coolest girls we've ever worked with, but right now the outside is not matching the inside."

Valeria shrugged. "I like it that way. I don't want it to seem like the only thing I care about is my looks."

Carmen nodded understandingly. "But, *chica,*

there's something between being too vain and, on the other hand, caring just enough to make sure your look communicates all the incredible things that are going on in your big, beautiful brain."

Jamie held up the iPod. "Like this Emily character. She doesn't play by the rules, but she's definitely got style."

Carmen perked up. "Hey, let me see that."

Jamie handed it over and Carmen held it up next to Valeria's face. "Check it out, y'all. How cute would this hairstyle be on her?"

Alicia tilted her head, her expression amused. "And how funny is it that it took you exactly three days in Texas to start saying 'y'all'?"

Valeria looked doubtful. "You do know that she's a graphic-novel character, not a real person . . ."

Alicia stood next to Jamie. She looked at the picture of Emily the Strange, then at Valeria, then back. "You know, it's genius, really."

"I think you *chicas* are amazing. But I don't know about this whole makeover thing. I haven't cut my hair since I was in the seventh grade."

"No offense," Jamie teased, "but it looks like it."

"Trust us," Carmen said. "As long as Alicia isn't your stylist, you're in safe hands."

"That's for sure," said Jamie. "Alicia decided to take it upon herself to give Sarita, our first *quince* client, a new hairstyle, and the poor girl wound up with a seriously bald spot. Alicia was going for the Natalie Portman look in *V for Vendetta*."

"I have to admit, it was pretty bad, and, trust me, I learned my lesson," Alicia chimed in. "I had to do some pretty serious groveling to keep Sarita from first firing me and then taking a contract out on my life."

"So, if we keep Alicia at a safe distance, are you game, V.?" asked Jamie.

"Why not?" Valeria replied, giving in. "I guess you only live once."

Alicia made a quick call to Mrs. Castillo to get the okay for Valeria to cut her hair. To which Mrs. Castillo replied, "Yes. Of course. Thank God."

After that, Jamie called her cousin Anton in New York and within minutes had the name of the best stylist in Austin; but when she called the salon for an appointment, they told her there was nothing available before the date of Valeria's *quince*.

"Okay, maybe this is a sign we should leave well enough alone," Valeria said, slumping onto the couch. "I could brush my hair. Condition it. Something."

"No way," Jamie insisted. "I'll call my cousin back.

Anton will make it happen." And he certainly did. An hour later, they had an appointment in Austin for the next day at eleven a.m.

"So it's really happening. Change is good, right?" a nervous Valeria asked.

Carmen held up the iPod with their inspiration image and said, "No, V. Change is *awesome*."

CHAPTER 10

IT WAS VALERIA'S turn to surprise the Miami girls. "I'll agree to the haircut with no complaints," she said the next morning when she greeted them. Then she held up a finger as Alicia started to speak. "*If* we go by the Rutherford Ranch skate park first. I want you to see a little more of my world before I get all into your makeover world."

"Fair enough," Alicia said, as they boarded the ranch van. "But our appointment is at eleven, and since it's a bit of a diva salon, we can't be late."

"No problem, it won't take long to show you how smooth I am on the half-pipe," Valeria replied, her tone unusually confident and sassy. Although she insisted that she wasn't into style, Alicia noticed she was wearing a hot pink T-shirt that said, LET'S PLAY TRIKTIONARY and green camo pants with matching green and pink sneaks.

They got to Rutherford Ranch to find a concrete park with half-pipes, bowls, fun boxes, and pyramids. Everyone seemed to know Valeria, and a couple of the guys even cleared off the quarter pipes to give her room.

"Looking good, Lady V.," said a very, *very* cute boy with sandy blond hair and the most amazing blue, almost violet, eyes, as soon as they entered the park. The three friends exchanged curious glances.

All thoughts of cute boys vanished as soon as Valeria started 'boarding, and the three friends tried to make sense of what she was doing; it appeared she was defying gravity. From the way the boys in the park were calling them out, the moves she was executing from her "triktionary" included: a Five-Oh grind, a Bert slide, and a 50-50. An hour later, the girls had forgotten about the time. . . .

Until Alicia looked at her watch and nearly freaked. "Yo, Valeria!" she yelled. "We've got to go."

Valeria gave her a thumbs-up, then did a vertical slide up a wall before getting off the rails.

"Wow!" Alicia said when Valeria joined them. "You weren't kidding when you said that skateboarding was your calling."

"Hey, Lady V., you were strictly diamonds out there today," said the same cute guy with the aforementioned blue-violet eyes as he walked over.

Valeria looked away, using her long hair to shield her face, and did a very effective impersonation of Cousin Itt from *The Addams Family*. "Hey, Omarion," she said softly. "Uh, this is Alicia, Jamie, and Carmen. They're from Miami."

Omarion shook hands with each of them. "Much respect, ladies. Any friend of V.'s is a friend of mine. Hope y'all enjoy Austin. It's special. Just like this lady here."

He walked away, and Carmen said, "Please tell me that you're dating that guy."

Valeria let out a very unladylike guffaw. "Omarion? Uh, no."

"Do you have something against hotties?" Jamie asked, staring at the guys as they flew around on their boards.

Alicia smacked Jamie's arm playfully. "Hello, you've got a boyfriend."

Jamie shrugged. "Yeah, but he's a little square. These guys have street style. They've got swagger."

"Oh, boy," Alicia said. "Look at what you've done, Valeria. She's back on the swagger thing again. It took her a long time to figure out that she should give the nice preppy boy a chance."

"Sorry," Valeria said, shrugging.

"No worries. Just messing with you," Alicia said. "But speaking of nice boys, who *is* your *chambelán*?"

Valeria looked less than enthused. "My cousin Bruno has agreed to be my nonthreatening date."

"But what about Omarion?" Jamie asked, staring as the boy ollied a twelve set. "He's so cute. Do you not like him?"

Valeria's hair covered her face like a curtain as she mumbled something.

"She likes him," Jamie said. "He's *got* to be your *chambelán*."

Alicia looked at her watch, "V., or Lady V., as Señor Hotness likes to call you, we don't have time for all this. One, if we don't leave this skate park in eight minutes, we'll be late for your very exclusive hair appointment. Two, your party is a week from Saturday. Ask him out."

"Or we will," Jamie said, glancing dreamily back at the skate park.

"Behave, Jamie!" Carmen warned.

"I meant, we'd ask him out on your behalf!"

"I've never done something like this before. You need to give me time to psych myself up," sighed Valeria. "I promise I'll call him later, when we get back to the ranch."

"Good girl!" Carmen cheered. "Now, let's go and make you presentable."

At exactly one minute to eleven, Valeria, Alicia, Carmen, and Jamie found themselves outside of the salon, Glitterati.

"I don't know if I'm ready," Valeria said, putting a strand of her hair into her mouth and chewing nervously.

Carmen grimaced. "Just the fact that you are *eating* your hair right now means that you are in a pitiful state."

"And remember, you said no complaints if we went to the park," Alicia reminded their client.

The salon, when they entered, was not what they expected. The customers were well-dressed Texan women in their forties and fifties—basically women who reminded them of their moms. But the stylists were another breed altogether. There were six of them in total, each wearing five-inch heels, neon catsuits, and hair that was teased to a point way past Crazy Anchor Lady.

The receptionist, whose name tag read CHARMAINE, was the most conservatively dressed, in a 1950s-style blue satin dress and a bun that was so high and full it seemed that bees might swarm out of it at any moment.

"Well, hello, young and beautiful," she said. "Which one of you fillies is Valeria?"

The *quince* of the moment stepped forward nervously, shoulders slumped, eyes firmly fixed on the ground. "That would be me."

Charmaine shook her head. "Oh, do not step to me like you're a soldier facing a firing squad," she said. "You're on the front lines of fabulous! I want you to strut!"

"I'm sorry," Valeria responded meekly. "I'll do better next time."

The receptionist scowled. "Not next time. This time. Go back to the front door, and then come up to me like you're a supermodel walking the runway."

Jamie, Alicia, and Carmen watched in stunned silence. No way was Valeria going to do it.

But they were in for a surprise.

Maybe it was because they'd spent the morning at the skate park and Valeria was 'board-happy. Maybe it was the thought that that hottie Omarion, maybe, just maybe, would agree to be her *chambelán*. Or maybe it was just the fact that Amigas Inc. had been boosting her confidence. Whatever it was, it seemed as if suddenly, shy Valeria had been replaced by a bolder version of herself. "Okay, why not?"

Valeria looked over at the other girls. "I think I need different shoes. May I borrow yours, Alicia? I think we're the same size."

Alicia nodded happily and sat down to take them off.

Valeria took off her combat boots and slipped on Alicia's platform shoes. Then she walked back out the door. A moment later it opened again, and she sashayed to the reception desk. Valeria tossed her hair and posed at the front desk with her hand defiantly posed on her jutting hip.

"OMG," Alicia said. "Who the heck was that?"

Jamie giggled. "I think it's Lady V., from the skate park."

Valeria blushed. "I watch a lot of modeling shows. It's my guilty pleasure."

Before they could grill her about what else she was hiding, a tall woman with big blond hair approached, saying, "Charmaine, are you teaching charm school again?"

Charmaine smiled. "Maybelline, meet your new client, Valeria. Take good care of her, because that girl is hiding a reservoir of *fierce*."

The girls followed Valeria and Maybelline to a chair in the back of the salon. Carmen handed Maybelline a picture of Emily the Strange. "This is our inspirational picture," she explained.

Maybelline took the photo. Carmen noticed that on each perfectly manicured fingernail there was a picture of an oil well.

"Oh, honey, I am my own inspiration," Maybelline said. "But I will take your wishes into account."

"Should we be worried?" Carmen whispered to Jamie.

"Nope," she said. "I think our Valeria is in excellent hands."

And she wasn't wrong.

An hour later, Maybelline waved a hair dryer around Valeria's head as if it were a magic wand. Emily the Strange might have been the starting point for the *quince*'s makeover, but there was nothing cartoonish about Valeria's final look. She had bangs, but they were fringed so that they seemed to have a little bit of rock-and-roll edge. The rest of her hair was shoulder-length, and it curled under ever so slightly, in a natural wave.

Maybelline had given Valeria a few midnight blue highlights that were amazingly subtle in her glossy jet black hair. As a finishing touch, she had trimmed and brushed Valeria's dark brows, which were now like gallery frames for her eyes.

The hairdresser spun the chair around so Valeria could see the back of her haircut. "I believe the term is *voilà*," she said.

"That's not me." Valeria sounded shocked. "That couldn't be me."

Maybelline gave her client a kiss on the cheek. "But is it ever, diva. Now, get out there and shine!"

As they left the salon, the three Miami girls jockeyed for credit for Valeria's new look. Walking down the street, even though she was still wearing her standard uniform—message T, camo pants, and skate sneaks—Valeria didn't look out of place next to the members of Amigas Inc. On the contrary, with her new haircut, it was as if she'd staked her own claim to the girls' stylish *glamocracy*.

"I do believe that I was the one who used the word *haircut* first," Alicia pointed out. "Maybe even at the airport when we first arrived."

"You're kidding, right?" Carmen said. "I was thinking about different hairstyles from the first night we got here."

Jamie shook her head. "I'm the one who saw the Emily iPod and said, 'Bam, that's the look.'"

Valeria laughed good-naturedly. "Okay, break it up.

I want to thank *all* of you for giving me this push out of my comfort zone. In fact, to thank you, I want to take you guys to my favorite *taquería* for lunch."

Alicia suddenly stopped short.

"What's wrong? You don't like tacos?" Valeria asked.

"No, that's not it." Alicia shook her head. Her eyes gleamed with excitement. This was a look that the other members of Amigas Inc. knew well. It was an inspired look. "I know what the theme for your *quince* should be. Your haircut gave me the idea. Valeria at Twilight! We have the church ceremony during the day. Then we have the party late that evening, say at ten p.m. And we serve a few hot appetizers, but the main course is a huge chocolate buffet. You said you love chocolate, right?" Valeria nodded and Alicia plowed on. "We really play with that intimate, late-night feeling. It's like you've invited your friends to your house, not for a big boring sit-down dinner, but for the main event—dancing, some sweets, and a chance to be with you as you blow your candles out at midnight. The clock strikes twelve, and it's your actual birthday. You're fifteen."

For a moment, no one said anything.

Finally, Valeria broke the silence. "I love it!" she cried.

"It is pretty fantastic," Carmen admitted.

Jamie did an elaborate bow before Alicia. "Your *quince* skills are unprecedented, madame."

Alicia flushed. Planning *quinces*. Traveling to a new city with your guy and your best friends. Dedicating yourself to reimagining and reinvigorating a Latina tradition. It didn't get any better.

Until . . . it got worse. *Much* worse.

Crossing the street, they walked by a café with a big picture window. "Hey, isn't that Gaz and Saniyah?" Jamie asked loudly.

Alicia stopped in her tracks and looked in at what was, indeed, her boyfriend through the window. And with him was Saniyah. She couldn't hear what they were saying, but it was clear they were laughing and having a good time. Anyone who saw them would have thought they were a couple.

"Isn't the conference on the other side of town?" Carmen asked. She looked mad, ready to defend her best friend.

"Let's not jump to conclusions," Jamie warned.

"Yeah," Valeria added. "Downtown Austin is actually really compact. They probably just came this way for lunch."

"Well, there's only one way to find out," Alicia said, pushing open the door of the café.

As the girls walked in, Alicia tried to calm her nerves. Although she tried not to go there, and even though Gaz had reassured her, seeing the two together made it so easy to picture Saniyah and Gaz as a couple. They just looked like they . . . belonged together.

Gaz stood up as she approached, looking unbothered. He gave her a kiss on the cheek. "Hey, fancy running into you here."

The girls exchanged hellos with Saniyah. "Your hair looks amazing," Saniyah said to Valeria. "Did you just get it cut?"

"Yeah, she did," said Alicia, answering for Valeria. "I thought you were at the conference. What brings you to this part of town?"

"Saniyah took me to the most incredible guitar shop," Gaz explained. "All the old-school Texas blues players used to hang out there. Guys like John Lee Hooker. It was pretty inspirational."

"In fact, we were just writing our own blues songs," Saniyah chimed in.

Gaz laughed. "Yeah, it's hilarious how easy it is. What they told us to do at today's panel was to begin the process of writing blues songs by just asking someone to give us a word. You got a word for me, Lici?"

Alicia bit her tongue. The first word that had come

to mind wasn't pretty. Plus, she couldn't help thinking that seeing Saniyah and Gaz had made her sad, and yet they were busting up laughing over the blues. "Sorry, can't think of any," Alicia said, shrugging.

Gaz looked at Jamie, oblivious of his girlfriend's unhappiness. "Okay, you give me a word."

"I'm hungry," Jamie said. "So, how about *pancakes?*"

Gaz nodded and reached for his guitar and began playing a basic blues melody. Then he began to sing.

> *Woke up this morning,*
> *Flapjacks on my mind.*
> *But my cupboards are empty,*
> *And I ain't got a dime.*
>
> *I got the blues.*
> *The pancake-dreaming*
> *Belly-empty*
> *Nothing-eating*
> *Kind of blues.*

Alicia wasn't used to seeing this new, outgoing Gaz. She wondered if Saniyah had brought this out in him or if it was just being at the conference, surrounded by music, that was doing it.

When the song was over, the girls clapped, joined

by some of the other patrons in the café.

"You just made that up on the spot?" Alicia asked, impressed in spite of herself. "That's pretty cool."

"That's what makes it so much fun," Gaz said. "The blues has some standard elements: 'Woke up this morning' and 'having a really miserable day' are two of them."

Saniyah wiggled in her seat. "Oooh, my turn. Pick a word. Any word. But it would help if it's a word that's easy to rhyme."

Alicia smiled not so sweetly and suggested, "Fire hydrant."

Saniyah took out her guitar. "Tough customer. Let me see what I can do."

She thought for a few moments. Then she began to sing.

> *Woke up this morning,*
> *In my Chevrolet,*
> *Parked next to a hydrant.*
> *Now they're towing me away.*
>
> *I got the blues.*
> *Why is life so unfair?*
> *Cop saw me sleeping.*
> *Should've just left me there.*

I got the
Car-impounded
Heart-is-pounding
Lover-left-me.
Life's-so-empty
Kind of blues,

Down deep in my soul.

The girls, even Alicia, along with Gaz, clapped for Saniyah.

"I'm playing tonight at a karaoke club," she said, laughing. "It's called the Tin Bucket. They're having an under-twenty-one night. Y'all should come."

"I'd love to!" Valeria said, still riding the wave of her new confidence. "It'll give me someplace to show off my new hair."

"Valeria can go," Alicia said, "but the rest of us have too much *quince* work to do."

"Come on," Jamie said. "All work and no play . . ."

"Makes for some very dull *amigas*," Carmen added, warming to the idea.

"Fine, fine," Alicia said. "We'll go. But we'll have to have a working dinner. If we don't focus more on the party, we're going to sink into some serious doo-doo."

"Great," Saniyah beamed. "I'll see you there."

• • •

Later that night, after dinner, the crew went to hear Saniyah play. On the way over, Jamie and Valeria sat up front in the van, discussing the new theme and possible decorations. Carmen sat farther back, furiously texting Domingo. And in the last row sat Alicia and Gaz, as far apart as possible—*not* holding hands and *not* kissing. And for a while, not talking.

"I just don't get it," Alicia finally said. Since running into Gaz and Saniyah, she'd been giving him the cold shoulder. She couldn't help it. It was a knee-jerk reaction. Part of her knew he would never cheat, and that he cared about her—a lot. But a teeny-tiny other part just couldn't see past the smile he had shared with Saniyah while he sang. "Since when are you into blues music?"

Gaz looked confused. "What kind of question is that? I'm a musician. I'm into music of all kinds. A good musician lets it all flow, gets in touch with his feelings and the people around him."

Alicia couldn't stop herself. All she could imagine was him getting in touch with Saniyah. Suddenly, she flipped.

"I'm really trying to be okay with this, Gaz, but I can't pretend that your hanging out all the time with

Austin's answer to Selena Gomez doesn't bother me. I saw the way you looked at her at the Hacienda." She blinked back tears and continued, "You like her because the two of you have so much in common."

Gaz looked as shocked by the outburst as Alicia was at having it. "Saniyah is a nice girl. She's helping me out a lot with the industry stuff. But I don't like her like that. I like *you*," he said.

Alicia mustered up a small, rueful smile. He honestly looked as though he meant it. Wiping the tears from her face, she thought, *then why doesn't it feel that way?*

The rest of the ride was silent, and by the time they got to the club, Alicia was actually looking forward to seeing Saniyah perform. Anything to put an end to this awkwardness. When they got inside, they saw a sawdust-covered floor. The unofficial uniform of the clientele seemed to be cowboy hats and Levis. Their jaws dropped.

"Welcome to your first honky-tonk," Valeria said.

Jamie, who was wearing a dress and high heels, smiled and said, "We stick out like sore thumbs. I love it. It's so easy to be renegade down here."

The group found a table near the stage, and, a few

minutes after they arrived, Saniyah came on. She was dressed like most of the audience, in a cowboy hat, a lavender pearl-buttoned shirt, and a pair of nondesigner jeans. "My name is Saniyah Camilo," she said, "and I'm a sophomore at Austin High. It's my pleasure to play a few songs for you tonight."

Alicia watched her take a seat on a high stool onstage. Saniyah seemed as comfortable as if she were sitting in her living room.

"We all know that Austin is the live-music capital of the world," Saniyah said, "but this week, because of South by Southwest, the city is overrun with visitors. I've had the pleasure of meeting a few new friends from Miami who are here tonight"—Saniyah waved at their table—"so I thought instead of showcasing my new, original music, I'd stick with some country classics and sing a few songs by Miss Patsy Cline."

There were loud whoops of appreciation from the audience, but the members of Amigas Inc. just looked blankly at one another. None of them were familiar with Patsy Cline.

"As the great Lyle Lovett would say," Saniyah continued, "Patsy Cline is not from Texas, but we love her anyway."

She began to sing, her voice rich and sweet. She

might have had a multioctave range, as Gaz had said, but that night, she stuck to her deepest register, belting out the songs with the force of someone who knew about heartbreak. When she was done, even Alicia had to join the room in giving her a standing ovation, no matter how much it killed her.

"Thank you, thank you," Saniyah said. "Now, enough of my squawking. This here's a karaoke joint, and we've got a whole jukebox of Texas favorites waiting for you to put your stamp on them."

Alicia jumped to her feet. "I'll sing!" she shouted. The urge to outshine Saniyah wouldn't let up, no matter how much Gaz had tried to reassure her.

Gaz, Carmen, and Jamie looked horrified.

Valeria watched Alicia bound up to the stage. "What fun!"

Carmen whispered, "Not for us."

Valeria looked confused. "What do you mean?"

"We don't let Lici sing," Jamie answered for her, "because, well, she's really bad at it."

Ignoring her friends' not-so-hushed whispers, Alicia walked across the stage, her stilettos clicking loudly against the wooden floor.

"Y'all hear that?" Saniyah asked the crowd. "It's a city slicker in pursuit."

Everyone laughed, and Alicia blushed. Saniyah adjusted the mike and introduced Alicia. "Ladies and gentlemen, put your hands together for Alicia Cruz."

The crowd clapped, and Saniyah asked, "What are you going to sing?"

"The guy you mentioned before, Lionel Loving," Alicia mumbled.

The audience snickered disapprovingly.

"Do you mean Lyle Lovett?" Saniyah asked.

Alicia nodded.

"Okay, what song?" Saniyah handed her a playlist.

Alicia studied it blankly.

"This really isn't going to be good, is it?" Valeria asked Gaz, suddenly nervous for her new friend.

"Oh, no, not at all," Gaz said.

Alicia handed the book back to Saniyah. "'Long Tall Texan.'"

Saniyah gave Alicia a bemused look, "Okay, Miami, let's see what you got." She gave Alicia the stool and exited the stage.

The music began to play, and every one of her friends waited for the first off-key note. But then she surprised them. Instead of trying to compete with Saniyah musically, Alicia turned her song into a spoken-word piece. It was a hilarious song about a Texas man and his love of his hat, his horse, and the simple pleasures of living in the Lone Star State. Rather than embarrassing Alicia, it made the audience see how much fun she was having being in Austin. When she finished the song, the room broke into thunderous applause.

Saniyah came back and joined her on center stage. "You ought to take it on the road."

"I might just do that," Alicia beamed.

"Hey, somebody, get that Miami girl a hat," the owner of the club called out.

Someone from the audience threw a white cowboy hat onto the stage and yelled, "She's not from Texas, but Texas loves her anyway."

Alicia picked up the hat and put it on her head. Speaking into the mike, she said, "Ladies and gentlemen, I'm a Miami girl born and bred, but tonight, I'm feeling some love for the Lone Star State of Texas."

CHAPTER 11

THE NEXT DAY, as planned, Gaz met up with Saniyah at the conference convention center. T-Bone Burnett, the famous songwriter and movie composer, was speaking that morning in the big lecture hall on the process of composing for film. With fellow songwriter Ryan Bingham, Burnett had won an Academy Award for Best Original Song for their country-and-western hit "The Weary Kind," featured in the movie *Crazy Heart*. The auditorium was packed. Saniyah greeted Gaz with a kiss on the cheek. "Hey, G., we better get in. There's a guy saving our seats, but they won't last for long. It's a madhouse in there."

Gaz was startled anew by the same guilt he felt every time Saniyah kissed him hello. She said it was a Southern thing and a music industry thing, and that much seemed to be true. Everywhere he looked, people were hugging and kissing hello. In the plaza of the conference center, he'd seen John Mayer hugging it out with the guys from *Entourage*. America Ferrera was exchanging *besitos* with Selena Gomez—Saniyah said they were going to be playing sisters in an upcoming film. And just to the right of the lecture hall door, Taylor Swift, Carrie Underwood, and T-Bone were having a massive group hug.

While Gaz told himself that a kiss on the cheek from Saniyah was no big deal, he knew that if Alicia had seen it, she would find it to be *quite* a big deal, even if the previous night a friendship had started to build between the two girls.

"Let's go in," Saniyah said again, pulling him by the arm.

"You go ahead. I'll find you," Gaz said. "Just have to make a quick phone call. To, uh, the band back home."

He wouldn't tell Saniyah, but the call was most definitely not to the band. He was supposed to make some calls for Valeria's *quince*. Alicia had put him in charge of special effects and tuxedo duty, in addition to the music. That meant he needed to find a smoke machine, black lights, and glow-in-the-dark paint that could easily be painted over for the walkway to Valeria's house. He'd done very little on the *quinceañera* front, and he had to remind himself, if it hadn't been for

Valeria's mom, he wouldn't even be at South by Southwest. He just needed to grab half an hour and make the calls.

"There's no time, *chico*," Saniyah said, looking exasperated. "It's South by Southwest. You come prepared. You come focused. One hundred and ten percent. Game on. Do you want a record deal, or do you want to be playing *quinces* your entire life?"

The words stung, on more than one level. He *didn't* want to be playing *quinceañeras* his whole life. And yet, for Alicia, the parties and the business were everything. He didn't want to have to choose between making Alicia happy and fulfilling his own dreams. But more and more of late, he was feeling pushed to make that choice.

Gaz mumbled, "Record deal."

"Good," Saniyah said with a sharp nod. "Then I have three words for you: T. Bone. Burnett. And three more: Oscar. Winning. Composer. And, oh, yeah, three more: King. Of. Nashville. And a final three: Move your butt."

Gaz sighed and followed Saniyah into the lecture hall. Alicia would understand. It was only a smoke machine. How hard would it be to get one? He'd start making calls as soon as T-Bone's lecture was over.

• • •

Back at the Castillo Ranch, the girls huddled around the kitchen table sipping *café con leche* sprinkled with milk chocolate shavings from supersize mugs.

"Valeria, you've got to invite Omarion to your party today," insisted Alicia. "It's now or never, girl."

"I'll dial," offered Jamie. "All you need to do is talk. I'd volunteer to do the talking, too, but I'm afraid my Texas twang would sound way too Bronx."

Valeria gulped, but she nodded.

If nothing else, Alicia mused, the girl was definitely getting bolder.

Picking up her cell, Valeria started to walk out of the kitchen. "Wish me luck," she said over her shoulder. "Or, better yet, wish me the skills to actually carry on a conversation."

A few minutes later she returned with a big grin on her face.

"So, what'd he say?" Alicia asked.

"I'm more curious about what *you* said," Jamie said, looking at Valeria.

"I said, we're having this crazy party next week. Latin tradition. Old-school rules. Boys escort girls, did he want to come?" Valeria said, as though she hadn't, just a few minutes ago, been panicked at even the thought of dialing.

Alicia shrugged. "I guess that about sums it up."

"And he said yes?" Carmen nudged.

"And he said yes," Valeria repeated, glowing.

There was a moment of silence, and then everyone started jumping up and down screaming. They shrieked and hugged and giggled like ten-year-old girls at a Jonas Brothers concert; Valeria was the loudest of all.

After that, as if by some Texas magic, all of the elements of the Valeria at Twilight *quinceañera* began to come together smoothly. Jamie, ever the realist, argued that it had nothing to do with magic. She claimed that Valeria's getting the skater boy of her dreams to be her *chambelán* had been the result of supermotivation—plain and simple.

Whatever the reason, that afternoon, Amigas Inc. went into high gear. With Valeria's help, Alicia finished up the seating plan, placed an order with the florist for black orchid corsages for Valeria's *damas*, and commissioned fifty ceramic centerpiece vases decorated with photos of Texas longhorn cattle. Each one was to be filled with a mixed array of Texas wildflowers, reflecting the colors of the state flag—bluebonnets, red prairie paintbrush, and white baby's breath.

Since the timing had always been tight, Carmen had gone ahead and ordered the fabric and patterns for the dresses Valeria would wear; she would fit it perfectly once the material arrived. But that still left the court. In a decision based on limited timing, Carmen was going to purchase the court dresses. After visiting six designer boutiques to do a "preshop," Carmen settled on Enrico's, a store she felt had dresses that were stylish, well cut, and distinctive enough to complement Valeria's gown.

Jamie, meanwhile, found a craft store that could special-order a stamp listing all the invitation details. Her plan was to use the stamp with glow-in-the-dark ink that could be seen only with a special black-light flashlight pen that would be included in each custom-made envelope.

She ordered the stamp on Tuesday, it arrived on Thursday, and the ranch drivers hand-delivered invitations to a hundred of Valeria's and her parents' nearest and dearest friends and relatives that Friday morning— another item on the to-do list, done.

By Friday at lunch, the Castillos' phone was ringing off the hook. And most of the calls weren't of the friendly variety. It seemed Valeria was causing quite a stir. Her cousins Loretta, Laura, and Lourdes were incensed that she was bringing her "Keep Austin Weird" motto into the sacredness of the *quinceañera*.

"Of course, one might argue that the mechanical bull Loretta rode at her *quince* sullied the tradition, too," Valeria pointed out after Loretta's mom had called—for the fifth time. "But who am I to say?"

Amigas Inc. had never seen such family dramatics. They had gone ahead and cleared it with Valeria's priest to do a small church ceremony the morning of her birthday, in order to keep the late-night-party theme but retain the traditional elements. However, the Castillos' extended family were far more difficult to appease than the Catholic Church.

By five thirty that afternoon, the kitchen was filled to capacity with a gaggle of Valeria's angry aunts, Amigas Incorporated's members, Alicia's mother, and Valeria and her mother.

"*Mija,*" said Ranya's sister-in-law Doña Tania. "What were you thinking sending out Day-Glo invitations that you can only see with some ridiculous special pen? Is this a party to celebrate a *quince,* or the opening of one of those rave clubs? This is what you get when you hire teenage amateurs to do a professional's job."

"Did you read the *Miami Herald* article about Amigas Inc.?" Ranya asked, not taking the bait. She passed out colored photocopies to each of the three aunts. *"These girls are experts at creating a refreshing mix of the old and the new,"* she read. "That's why I invited them here to Austin. And that's why I trust them."

Doña Giselle, the oldest of the sisters, looked like a Latina Mrs. Claus. "We have *quinceañera* planners here in Texas," she said in a raspy drawl. "You had to bring these young party-minded girls from Miami? I couldn't even read my invitation without a flashlight. I don't like it. It's not tradition."

Doña Griselda, the mother of the *quince* who had worn the Texas flag panties, wasn't going to be left out. "And look at Valeria's hair. It's very radical. She looks like something out of a music video. It's immoral. I do not like it."

Carmen had to restrain herself from making a biting retort. Had the woman looked in the mirror lately?

She was dressed like an Italian widow in a black lace dress, complete with veil and little black gloves. ("This, despite the fact that my uncle is very much alive," Valeria had whispered to them when the older woman had first arrived.)

"And who ever heard of a *quince* starting at ten p.m.?" added Doña Tania, now looking at her sisters and not at Valeria or her mother. "Valeria at Twilight? I don't like it."

The aunts sat around the kitchen table, not touching

the cups of coffee that Ranya had poured for them and glaring at Valeria and her new friends. Mrs. Cruz stood next to Ranya, arms folded, ready to jump in if necessary. But Valeria's mother had it covered.

"Okay, I've had enough," Ranya said, leaning across the kitchen table and staring the aunts down. "Let me be perfectly clear. It doesn't matter what *you* like. It's not your *quinceañera*, it's Valeria's, and I think the *amigas* are doing an amazing job. The invitations are *meant* to evoke a nightclub feeling. These are teenagers. They go out at night, sometimes to clubs. If you had read your invitations rather than just criticized them, you would have seen that we are having the religious service during the day. Our church okayed the late party start. Who are you to overrule the church? The *quince* is starting at ten p.m. because it's a dessert party."

Valeria piped up, "And I'm a vegetarian—a fact none of you remembered to take into account when you planned your daughters' *quinces*, and I was forced to survive on wilted lettuce leaves and salad plates full of white rice."

Valeria's aunts began muttering among themselves, but Ranya was far from done. "Listen closely," she said. "I've had enough of this. I *love* Valeria's haircut. It's the first time in a long time that I can look into my beautiful daughter's eyes. In a few days, my daughter will be turning fifteen. We sincerely hope that you will be there. But right now we've still got a lot of work to do, so I'm going to have to ask you to leave and let us do our job."

Alicia lifted her hands to clap, but her mother grabbed and stilled them in the nick of time. The Doñas were done for. It would have added insult to injury for the Miami crew to throw in their applause.

Doña Giselle looked at her watch. "I have an appointment with my facialist," she said.

Doña Griselda added, "I have to go pick up my daughter from cheerleading practice."

Doña Tania did not make excuses. She simply went up to Valeria, hugged her, and said, "I'll pray for you, child."

Then all three aunts left the room. Only then, finally, did Alicia offer a small round of applause. After all, Ranya, and Valeria, deserved it.

Things were coming together—minus some unhappy aunts—but that didn't mean the team could slack off. Which was why, that Saturday at breakfast, Valeria shocked them by announcing that she had to go to school. When the other girls raised their eyebrows,

Valeria explained that every Saturday, she and a bunch of her friends from the Ann Richards School met with seventh grade girls from poorer neighborhoods in Austin for three hours of tutoring. Then they all went out for barbecue. Valeria said that not only was it incredibly fun, but the girls had all improved more than forty percent on their reading and math scores since the program had started.

Though Alicia, Carmen, and Jamie still looked uncertain—and Alicia also looked panicked at the idea of losing a half day of *quince* planning—Valeria invited them to come along and do a presentation about *quinceañera* culture. "It would be the perfect thing for these girls to hear. How the *quinceañera* gives young Latina women a chance to step up in their communities, and how Amigas Inc. has made you guys into leaders."

It was hard to argue with that logic. Smiling, Alicia nodded. "Let's go meet ourselves some future customers—or business partners!" she announced.

Once at the school, the girls got to see another side of Valeria—a side that was coming out more and more as the day of her *quinceañera* approached. She might have started out on the reserved side, but it was clear that in this environment she was no shrinking violet. This was doubly true when it came to her mentee, twelve-year-old StarKeisha. "StarKeisha really wants to go to the Ann Richards School in the ninth grade," Valeria explained, "but she has a long way to go in terms of getting her grades up. If I can help her, well, then I've done my job."

After settling the Amigas group in, Valeria rounded up the students and mentors and brought them into the school auditorium for the featured presentation. Thanks to the wonders of YouTube, and with the help of a laptop and a projector screen, the girls were able not only to tell the Tejanos about *quinces* in Miami, they were able to *show* them as well. It was, without a doubt, a huge hit. After fielding at least two dozen questions, the presentation finally came to a close, and Alicia, Carmen, and Jamie were able to sit back and just observe. It was amazing to watch the younger girls light up, even when being challenged to push their intellectual limits or move out of their comfort zone.

And the mentors were impressive as well. They put up with the occasional attitudes and eye rolls and went with the flow, just eager to make a difference in these girls' lives.

As Alicia watched, her mind started racing; an idea was forming. An idea that had some great potential. Finally, she couldn't keep it bottled up any longer.

Since everything in Texas was bigger and better, why not double the traditional number of girls in Valeria's court and turn the seven mentees into a court of junior *damas*, who would play a special role in Valeria's *quinceañera*? When she suggested it, Valeria flipped.

Of course, that meant juggling things and more planning. But, Alicia thought, that is what we do best.

CHAPTER 12

EVERYTHING HAD been going smoothly—too smoothly. Alicia, always one to be nervous and worried, was waiting for the inevitable moment when things would go wrong. And with less than a week till Valeria's *quinceañera*, they did. True, certain things were all set. The catering was being handled by the Fat Turkey Chocolate Company, and Jamie was almost done with the decorations. Alicia had all the seating plans arranged and had even managed to figure out how to give the *tías* the best seats in the house without upsetting anyone else.

But Carmen was in trouble. Unless she could find some really talented elves, Valeria's junior *damas* would have either no dresses or, at best, ill-fitting ones on the big day. There was just no way that she alone could buy and do the alterations on seven more dresses in less than a week. Her fingers were already raw from working on Valeria's dresses, which, while hip and amazing, were not made from the easiest fabrics to cut.

And while Valeria's church had signed off on the late-night *quince*, the *amigas* were pretty sure that presenting Valeria's junior court in their birthday suits would not be appreciated.

That morning at breakfast, Carmen finally gave in. No matter how much she wanted to do everything, she was just one girl. One girl with very painful fingers and eyes that had been squinting for so long she was pretty sure they would never open again.

"I'm going to need some help, *chicas*," she announced. "Valeria's entrance dress is done, but I've only got five days to finish up her traditional dress, I still have to get final measurements from the *damas*—who I'm hoping won't lie to me about their sizes—and then make those alterations. And with the addition of the junior *damas* to dress, it's impossible."

"I feel your pain," Valeria said, sipping a cup of Aztec chocolate. "Well, not exactly, because I don't sew. But I've seen how much sewing you've been doing, and I know this is a phenomenal amount of work. Mom and I were talking about it last night, and we had a thought. What if we tried to hire some additional seamstresses from the Austin community to help you with everything? I know it would be a bit extra, but Mom says we have the budget."

Carmen considered the idea, but looked worried. "I like it in theory. But we'd need miracle seamstresses who can stitch like the wind."

Valeria handed Carmen a business card. "Miranda's is the best fabric shop in town," she said. "Would you mind just taking a ride over there to see if there's anyone they recommend? If you can't find anybody, we'll figure out another solution—like me and Mom learning how to sew overnight."

A few hours later, Alicia and Jamie were in the Castillos' great room, discussing the china and linen rentals. The family was used to throwing big parties. But once the guest list climbed past one hundred, it was always easier and cheaper to rent plates, glasses, silverware, and tablecloths. They were in the middle of a heated debate over ivory versus cream when Carmen rushed into the room, looking as if she were ready to burst.

"That was probably the coolest experience *ever!*" she announced.

"What did you buy?" Alicia asked, gesturing toward the large bags in Carmen's hands.

Carmen threw the bags on the floor and plopped down on a couch. "I bought lots of fabric," she said. "Mexican stuff that I've never seen in Miami. But that's not what's important. What's *important* is who I met. I don't want to ruin the surprise. But suffice it to say that the great *dama* dress dilemma has been solved."

The next morning, the girls—including Valeria—were enjoying a late breakfast as they tried to relax before the rush started. But it was impossible. Every time the doorbell rang, or someone walked by, or they heard a knock on the door, Carmen leapt up. Finally, right when Alicia was about to staple her feet to the floor, the doorbell rang again, and Carmen's surprise visitors arrived. She got up again and gestured for Jamie and Alicia to join her in the entrance foyer.

Three older women stood outside the front door. They each had pincushion bracelets on their wrists and bags full of needles, thread, and other sewing materials dangling from each elbow.

"Amigas Inc., meet Abuelas Inc.," Carmen said, grinning.

"You're kidding about the name, right?" Alicia said.

The apparent manager of the group smiled and replied, "Why would we kid? It's a very good name.

And I think the Abuelas have been in business for a few more years than the Amigas!" She handed Alicia a business card.

ABUELAS INC.

SEAMSTRESSES FOR HIRE

WE SPECIALIZE IN WEDDINGS AND *QUINCES*.

"I'm Mia," she said, reaching out to shake hands with Alicia and Jamie. "I'm in charge of all our sub-contractors and business affairs."

"I'm Celia. I'm the head seamstress, and I do most of the design work," said the tall, elegant woman next to her, who looked so much like Carmen that she could have been her grandmother.

"*Mucho gusto*, I'm Adelita," said the sassy *abuela*. Carmen and Alicia exchanged glances. They both thought that Adelita was a back-to-the-future version of Jamie.

"So, Carmen says you can help her?" Alicia asked once the introductions were over.

Mia nodded. "It will be a piece of cake. We'll take care of as much as we can—or, should I say, Celia will—and then we'll delegate the rest to several seamstresses in the area," she explained. "Today's Monday;

we can deliver the dresses by Thursday at noon. It's cutting it close, but it still leaves us a little time to fix any catastrophes—like *damas* who may have fudged on their sizes."

Alicia was in awe. "Thursday afternoon would be perfect. I can't believe you can work so fast."

Carmen leaned over. "We needed miracle seam-stresses with Wonder Woman–fast sewing machines, and I found them."

Just then, Alicia's cell phone rang, and she excused herself. Five minutes later, she walked back into the great room, her face a mask of fury.

"Carmen, Jamie, may I see you in the kitchen?" she said through clenched teeth.

The minute they were out of earshot of the *abuelas*, Alicia screamed, "That was Omarion! He's at the tuxedo rental shop with the other *chambelanes*—and no Gaz! *Gaz* has the cashier's check for the tuxedo deposit! The tailors won't even measure the *chambelanes* without it." She began pacing back and forth, her breath uneven and her face red. "Would it be okay if I threw some-thing?" she asked, clenching her fists. "I really want to throw something."

A panicked Jamie looked around the room for something unbreakable. She grabbed two pot covers from where they were drying on the rack. "Here, bang these together."

Alicia banged the pots together, then put them down. "That didn't help at all. I just feel like a five-year-old."

Jamie shrugged. "Well, *chica*, I tried. . . ."

Carmen tried to remain calm. "I know you're upset, Alicia, but I'm sure he has a good reason."

Alicia had a nasty retort right on the tip of her tongue when Valeria entered the kitchen. "Is everything okay?" she asked. "I thought I heard banging."

Jamie handed her the two pot covers. "Guaranteed to relieve the *quince*-planning stress."

Alicia's cell phone rang again. She looked at the number and saw it was Gaz's. Sitting down on the kitchen floor, she leaned against the door of the fridge and flipped open the phone.

"Gaz, where are you?" she asked, not bothering to sound nice. She listened, a scowl on her face. "I don't *care* if your panel ran overtime. You've got the cashier's check for the tuxes. All of those guys were waiting for *you*. You've been spending all of your time with Saniyah and have done pretty close to nothing for this *quince*, which was why Valeria's parents paid to fly you here in the first place."

She listened in silence. "Okay, okay, fine," she said after a moment. Then she hung up.

The other girls looked at her expectantly.

"It's really not that easy to eavesdrop on only one side of the conversation," Jamie said. "I hate to ask, but, what did he say?"

Alicia threw up her hands and shrugged. Her voice was quiet, resigned, a little sad. "He's really sorry— bla, bla, bla. He's got this new artist showcase on Wednesday—bla, bla, bla. After that, he'll give us his undivided attention—bla, bla, bla."

"I think Saniyah is a bad influence," Carmen said.

"Let's not bring her up," Jamie suggested.

"I'm just saying . . ." Carmen continued. "The real problem is that Gaz is losing Alicia's trust."

"I think he's telling me what I want to hear," Alicia said. "I think he cannot fathom that *quinces* are as important to me as his music is to him. But what am I going to do? I love him—bla, bla, bla."

She turned away so that her friends wouldn't see just how close she was to tears.

No one said anything until finally, softly, she added, "He knew he was coming here to work on Valeria's *quince*. Amigas Inc. is a serious business and something we're actually making money from doing. How important can this conference or this gig really be to Gaz? I don't buy that it's all about the music. Honestly, do you think he would have been this irresponsible if he hadn't met Saniyah?"

CHAPTER 13

THE DAY OF Gaz's new-artist showcase, he woke hours before the alarm went off.

Going downstairs, he poured himself a cup of coffee and sat at the kitchen table, studying his lyrics. He'd written all the songs, but he was so nervous he worried he'd forget his own words. He'd already seen it happen that week at the conference. Just the day before, a guy had gotten up to perform at a showcase and flubbed his lines—not once, but twice.

Watching that guy choke and blow his one chance to impress the music-industry pros at the conference, Saniyah had given Gaz some good advice: "Focus on the melody." She followed that advice up with, "Let the guitar lead, because your fingers are stronger and surer than your voice will ever be. When I sing, I'm really paying most attention to the guitar. My voice is just along for the ride."

He just hoped he would remember that when the spotlight was on him.

To distract himself from what was going to happen later, he showered and dressed as quietly as he could. He looked at the hall clock. Six fifteen. Still plenty of time to catch the antelopes. He paused before Alicia's door. He wanted to wake her, get her to walk with him, make sure that she saw that he was wearing the shirt she had given him for good luck. He raised his hand to knock, but let it fall. There'd been nothing but frostiness between them since he had missed his appointment with the *chambelanes*. She hadn't even given him the shirt in person. She'd left it on his bed the night before with a note that just said, *I believe in you*. None of her typical *x*'s and *o*'s.

He couldn't completely blame her. He *had* been slacking off on his responsibilities. He hadn't rehearsed the *cumbia* song he was supposed to play on his guitar for Valeria's father-daughter *vals*. He hadn't listened to any of the ninety-five feminist goth songs that Valeria had loaded onto an iPod for him to help him figure out the musical theme. But he wasn't like Alicia—how she kept so many things going at once was nothing short of a mystery to him. She handled it all, from budgets and schedules to choreography and supplies.

He was different. He needed to do one thing at a

time. He knew how much he owed the Castillo family, and he would start pulling his weight as soon as he got through this one make-or-break day.

Stepping outside, he took in the morning that was still so dark it felt closer to night than day. He had a thermos of hot chocolate and the flashlight, and his guitar, strung over his shoulder. He found his spot on the bench and felt himself relax. His spot. He'd been in Austin for exactly ten days, and yet the ranch felt like a second home.

In the stillness of the new day, he took a sip of cocoa, then began to play his guitar—running through his songs softly and sweetly until the antelopes breezed past him and the sun revealed itself lazily in the sky.

By the time Alicia woke up at eight, Gaz was long gone. She texted him: *See you there.* Buena suerte. *Good luck.* And she told herself that she was being oversensitive in thinking that his one-word response (*thanks*) was cold.

Valeria's *quince* was just three days away, and Alicia knew from experience that this was the time to check and double-check the details. There were going to be a half dozen veggie appetizers to supplement the chocolate buffet. Jamie had done a charcoal portrait of Valeria with her new haircut, and Alicia had sent it out to be printed on two hundred paper cups and two hundred napkins. Even when you paid extra for rush service, you never knew if a package would turn up on time. Alicia had been tracking the cups and napkins on the UPS Web site on her cell phone from almost the moment she woke up. She breathed a sigh of relief when the doorbell rang at eleven a.m. and she saw the driver walk in with her two giant boxes.

Once that was settled, she began calling around about additional DJ equipment. Gaz would be DJ-ing largely using speakers plugged into his laptop, but Alicia always thought it looked best when a full DJ stand was set up, ready to go if Gaz felt inspired to throw in a CD that wasn't on the original mix or if a guest made a special request. Of course, Gaz had yet to give Valeria the tracks list to sign off on, but they could take care of that quickly. It was Wednesday; the party was Saturday. He'd get it done. She looked at her watch. Twelve thirty p.m. She had a meeting downtown with the pastry chef at one thirty, which would leave her plenty of time to get to Gaz's showcase by three.

At least, she *should* have had plenty of time.

Things started to unravel during the drive downtown. It took longer than she'd planned to get from the ranch to the *panadería*. Then, when she got there, she was told that the pastry chef, Noreen, was running a little late. On top of that, he had mistaken her order for someone else's, and she had to review all the items on the menu with him all over again. She chewed her lip nervously and kept her eye on her watch. Despite the setbacks, Alicia was sure she was not more than fifteen minutes behind schedule, and she was confident that she could make it on time.

Luis dropped her at the conference center at two forty-five. Still plenty of time. She went right to the visitors' desk to get a map so she wouldn't get lost. But the conference center was a maze. Simultaneous events were taking place in four different locations. Breathless, she ran toward the annex that housed the new artists' showcase. By the time she finally made it to the courtyard where Gaz was playing, the crowd was clapping, and he was walking off the stage. Saniyah was sitting in the front row cheering. She made eye contact with Alicia, a distinct look of disapproval flashing over her face.

Normally, that would have bothered Alicia. But not now. She had no right to be mad at Saniyah. The girl had made it to support Gaz, who wasn't even her boyfriend. And Alicia? She had missed his event.

Her stomach was in knots. This was the worst thing that could have happened. Especially as things weren't exactly great between them. She was going to have to do some pretty good explaining, not to mention issuing a ginormous apology. But when she went up to speak to him, he gave her a huge hug, and her resolve vanished.

"What did you think, Lici? Amazing, right? I was only supposed to sing two songs. Then, you saw that guy in the blazer who came up to talk to me? He's one of the conference organizers. He told me to go ahead and play another one."

Alicia hugged him tightly. He obviously thought she had seen his performance. "That is great! Of course, you were good," she said, hoping he couldn't see through her lie.

He kissed her. "It wasn't me. It was my lucky shirt and my incredible girlfriend. I wouldn't even be here without you."

She looked around and realized there must have been two hundred people jammed into the courtyard. Gaz hadn't seen her come in.

How could she tell him the truth?

After dinner, later that night, Saniyah surprised everyone by showing up at the house. The Miami crew was sitting around the kitchen of the guesthouse eating homemade prickly pear sorbet. At the sight of Saniyah, Alicia's heart raced. Was she here to rat Alicia out to Gaz?

Luckily, that wasn't her reason for stopping by. "Hey, Valeria," Saniyah said. "I just stopped by to give you this. It's a little birthday present. Gaz was telling me about the girls you mentor and how much this tradition means to you, and I was just so inspired I wrote a song about it, about you. It's called '*Hermanas.*'"

Valeria stood up and gave Saniyah a hug. "Oh, my God, thank you! Will you perform it at my *quince*?"

Saniyah laughed and looked down at her feet. "Come on, you haven't heard it yet. It could suck."

Valeria shook her head. "I haven't heard the song yet, but I've heard you. Your voice is so beautiful. It would be an honor for me if you would sing at my *quince*."

Saniyah looked touched. "Well, when you put it that way, I'd love to. My mom is actually waiting in the car for me, so I'd better go. Good night, everyone."

Valeria nodded. "I'll walk you out. I should head back up to the house anyway. *Buenas noches*, everyone."

She left, and Jamie went up to the room the girls shared to work on her special video project. Carmen went off to text Domingo. Soon, Alicia and Gaz were the only ones left in the kitchen. Alicia began to clear the table. "How about you wash and I dry?"

"Or you could wash and I'll dry."

Alicia held up her hands. "Brand-new manicure. I dry." Then, turning to him, she said, "That's pretty cool that Saniyah wrote a song for Valeria."

"I didn't even know she was working on it," Gaz said, nodding. "I can't wait to hear it."

"Well, it does pose the question of why you've never written a song about me," Alicia said teasingly.

Behind her, she heard the glass break. Whirling around, she saw Gaz standing over the broken dish. He looked confused and hurt.

"What's wrong?" Alicia asked, concerned. "Are you okay?"

"I *did* write a song about you: 'Playing for Keeps,'" Gaz said. "It was the first song that I sang today. If you'd been there, like you *said* you were, you would've heard it."

Alicia started to stammer. "Well, I was there. You saw me. You know how spread out everything is there. I was a little late. I must have missed the first song."

Gaz leaned against the counter and crossed his arms. "How late? Did you hear the second or third song?"

Alicia shook her head.

"Why did you lie?"

Not knowing what to say and fearing that her mouth had already gotten her into a lot of trouble, Alicia said nothing at all.

That was all Gaz needed to hear—or not hear. He turned and walked out of the house. Alicia wanted to follow him, but what would she have said? "Sorry" wouldn't cut it. Not now. Not after how royally she had messed up. So she did what her mother always advised—she controlled the controllable. She got a broom and a dustpan and began to sweep up the broken glass.

Later that night, Jamie and Carmen went out to hear a local band, leaving Alicia in the guest room wondering how things had become such a big mess. Her eyes were red and puffy from hours of crying, but she didn't care. Who was going to see her like this, anyway? Suddenly, there was a knock at the door, and Valeria entered.

"Hey, how's it going?" she asked.

Alicia straightened up and tried to pretend that she hadn't just been crying. "Everything's great," she said, trying to smile brightly. "Your *quince* is going to be amazing."

Valeria shook her head. "I know it will be great. That's not what's worrying me. But I *am* worried about you and Gaz. It seems like you guys are in a rough patch."

Alicia sighed. "I lied to him. I got caught. Life pretty much sucks right now."

Valeria smiled gently. "You know, in Texas, we have a healthy respect for the tall tale. You may have told a lie, but he's been stretching the truth, too."

Alicia's eyes widened. "Do you think he's been cheating on me with Saniyah?"

Valeria put a reassuring arm around her new friend's shoulder. "Oh, my goodness, no. I just mean I think Gaz has been fooling himself by pretending that his heart is in Amigas Inc. You know, there's another saying, you can't dance at two weddings with one tush."

Alicia nodded slowly, as understanding dawned. "He can't be in the *quince* business *and* the music business at the same time."

"Exactly. But just like you need him to forgive you, he needs you to give him an out," Valeria said. "Why don't you invite him to go on a boat ride tomorrow? Riding around Lake Austin in a canoe is one of the best cure-alls I know."

Alicia looked at Valeria. "You're pretty wise for someone who hasn't turned fifteen yet."

"Well, we're just generally more advanced down

here in Texas," Valeria joked, giving Alicia a hug. "Big hats, big cattle, big brains . . . big hearts."

Gaz seemed hesitant when Alicia asked him to take a ride out with her to Lake Austin the next morning. But he softened when she added, "If we're going to be well and truly done, let's make sure we finish things right."

"I'm not saying we're done," he whispered.

"Good, then come out with me."

They didn't say much on the ride over. But their eyes widened as they walked down the path to the boat-rental shack. The lake was big and beautiful, and they felt as if they were walking through a painting.

Alicia paid for the rental, and she and Gaz pulled the boat into the water, laughing a little as they tried to steady it and get in.

"The urge to throw you in is so huge," Gaz grinned.

"And I completely deserve it," Alicia added. "But as I didn't bring a change of clothes, I'm going to beg you to take it easy on me."

"Maybe," Gaz said.

"I'm sorry I lied to you," Alicia said when they had paddled away from the shore. The lake was still and peaceful. "Not my finest moment, and it won't happen again."

"I want to believe you. . . ." Gaz began.

"So, believe me," Alicia insisted. "Because I need you to know that, as much as I want us to do everything together, including planning *quinces*, and going to school, and hanging out, and talking about music the way you do with Saniyah, I *finally* get it. Just like I eat, sleep, and breathe *quinces*, music is *your* everything. You should focus on that. I'm not a musician. I don't know a lot about the industry, so I can't say I'll be a huge help with your career. But I can tell you that if you let me, I'll be in the front row each and every time."

Gaz was silent for a long time, and Alicia felt her heart pounding.

And then he spoke.

"So, no more Amigas for me?"

She nodded.

"And you'd basically be my groupie?" he asked, mischievously.

"Something like that," Alicia said.

"Will you wear a T-shirt with my picture on it?"

"Absolutely."

"Memorize all the lyrics to all my songs?"

"Done."

"Will you make sure I have only blue M&M's in my dressing room?"

Alicia raised an eyebrow.

Gaz shrugged. "I read some bands have got crazy riders in their contract like that. Only blue M&M's. Only orange Fanta in the fridge. Stuff like that."

Alicia sighed. "When you start performing at places with a dressing room, then, yes, I will be on M&M duty."

Gaz conceded. "Then I think we can officially consider ourselves made up."

Alicia shook her head. "No. Uh-uh. Not yet."

"Why not?"

Alicia answered, "Because there will be no making up without the make-up make-out."

Gaz smiled. "No problem." Then, balancing the canoe ever so carefully, he leaned over and kissed her.

Sighing, Alicia lost herself in the moment. This, she thought, is how it should always be. And while she hated fighting, she was glad they were back on the same page—and maybe even stronger than before.

CHAPTER 14

THE MØRNING of Valeria's *quince*, Gaz and Alicia woke up superearly and went out to see the antelopes do their morning ritual. Sitting on the bench, sipping from their thermoses, they looked at each other with the shared wonder of two people who knew how different life could be when you changed the scenery.

"I can't believe it's been only two weeks," Alicia said as she watched the blesbok do their wide-legged splits, as elegant as ballet dancers, across the field.

"I feel like a whole different person," Gaz admitted.

"Well, you are wearing jeans and cowboy boots," Alicia said playfully.

Gaz turned to her, suddenly serious. "I really am sorry I left you hanging with so much *quince* work."

Alicia waved dismissively. "Water under the bridge—or canoe." She smiled. "It's okay."

"It's not, really," he said. "But, as always, you've done

an amazing job. Valeria already has that post-*quince* glow—and she hasn't even had her party yet. Saniyah's song—about *hermanas* and women who mentor—that could be about you. You, Carmen, and Jamie are like the antimean girls. You meet a girl and you don't just plan a party, you figure out all these ways to make her life better. You're the definition of a *hermana*."

Alicia looked at Gaz, amazed at all he'd said, all he'd noticed over the past year of her work with Amigas Inc. She wondered if that were the definition of love—to be seen in all these lovely ways by someone you didn't even know was watching.

They walked arm in arm back to the big house. For their penultimate Texas breakfast, Jamie reprised her Amigas *migas*—serving up hearty portions of eggs, crunchy tortilla strips, and spicy chorizo. They were just finishing up breakfast and about to work out getting all fourteen members of the court primped and pretty with only one bathroom and an hour to spare, when Valeria, still in her robe, burst into the guesthouse kitchen.

"Y'all have to see this," she said. "One of the cows is having a baby! Follow me."

She ran out toward the main barn, letting the screen door slam behind her.

"What did she just say?" Carmen asked.

Jamie smiled. "I think she just said that they're having a cow."

Gaz shook his head. "No, I think what she said is, 'Don't have a cow.'"

"Well, whatever she did or did not say, I think we need to go to the barn."

Quickly, everyone put on their shoes and coats and headed out.

"Do you think this is going to take long?" Alicia asked as they walked. "I'm all for the miracle of life, but we're due at the church for Valeria's *quince* blessing in two hours. I don't want to keep the priest—or her *loca* aunts—waiting."

Jamie gave her a look. "Seriously, *chica*," she said. "You think any of us knows about baby cows?"

Alicia laughed. They most certainly did not. But it would seem they were about to find out.

In the barn, several ranch hands held up gas lamps. Alicia's mom stood next to Ranya and David Castillo. The *amigas* and Gaz stood right behind Valeria. The expecting cow lay in the corner, away from the herd.

"Who could blame her for wanting a little privacy?" Alicia whispered.

"Do you see how her sides are inflating?" Valeria asked. "She's holding her breath."

The cow didn't do much for a full twenty minutes. Then she stood on her feet, and when she did, they could see the calf's nose sticking out. She let out a low moan.

Gaz looked as though he were about to lose his breakfast. "Oh, this is more than I want to know."

"Man up!" Alicia said. "How do you think you got here?"

"I just can't watch," he groaned, turning away, not embarrassed at all that the girls wanted to watch and he just couldn't.

Then the cow lay down on her side, and her moaning got more intense. They saw the calf's head, then her shoulders, then her whole body bounding out, with all of the energy of a newborn puppy.

Valeria clapped. "Okay, Gaz, it's safe for you to open your eyes now. She's just going to lick and clean her for a while."

For a moment there was nothing but awed silence as everyone took in the miracle in front of them. The baby was small yet strong, standing up right away to find milk. It was something none of them could have imagined, yet they wouldn't have missed it for the world.

Finally, everyone clapped, and the ranch staff popped open bottles of champagne and sparkling cider.

While they would have liked to stay and celebrate, there was another show that had to go on. Alicia looked at her watch and announced, "Hey, everybody, we have to shower, get dressed, and get out of here."

Valeria didn't look concerned. "No biggie," she said. "The church is just down the road."

Alicia put her hand on Valeria's shoulder. "*Chica*, I think you're awesome. But after spending two weeks in Texas, I've determined that nothing—and I do mean nothing—is '*just down the road.*'"

She turned back to the barnful of gawkers. "Okay, everybody. I need you dressed and waiting by the vans in thirty minutes. Let's get Valeria to the church on time!"

Ranya whispered to Marisol, "Were we ever that commanding in high school?"

Marisol said, "I wasn't, but . . ."

From across the room, Alicia smiled sweetly at her mom, then jerked a thumb at the barn door. "Keep it moving, Mom. There's plenty of time to chat in the car."

Ranya and Marisol giggled like teenagers and saluted Alicia military style as they hurried out the door.

• • •

When they arrived at the cathedral, Carmen, Jamie, and Alicia saw that all of the guests were seated and waiting. Taking the lead, Alicia told the crowd, "Our *quinceañera* is on her way. Valeria and her father were delayed due to the birthing of a baby calf. You all are from Texas. I'm sure you understand."

There was applause from the appreciative audience, and then a stunned silence as Valeria emerged in the doorway of the church. Omarion sat in the front row, and from the gaga expression on his face, the *amigas* could tell that Valeria's crush was most definitely requited. Maybelline and Charmaine from the hair salon sat in the fifth row, whispering, "Work it, sister!" and "Fierce. Absolutely fierce," as Valeria strutted down the aisle.

While the *amigas* had planned dozens of *quinces*, they had never seen a transformation as complete as Valeria's. From Valeria the geek—matted, greasy hair covering her eyes, a Keep Austin Weird T-shirt, and a gaze glued to the floor as if it were the most fascinating thing ever—to Valeria the chic—stunningly dressed, perfectly cut bangs, and loose waves that framed her heart-shaped face.

Carmen had outdone herself with Valeria's church dress: classic white, with yellow embroidery along the bodice and the hemline of the skirt symbolizing the Yellow Rose of Texas. As Valeria glided down the aisle, the *amigas* could hear the oohs and aahs of the crowd. Even Valeria's aunties had to admit their *sobrina* had never looked so amazing; she'd taken the whole Texas *quince* to another level.

But Valeria wanted to show her family and friends that no matter how slick her hair and makeup might be, she was still, deep down inside, the same Austin rock-and-roll girl. Instead of the demure flats that most *quinces* wore, Valeria wore yellow skate shoes. And instead of stilettos, which would have symbolized her walk into womanhood, Valeria's parents presented her with a pair of vintage leather cowboy boots.

In place of the usual crown on her head, her parents gave her a custom-made black cowboy hat with a hot pink lining. Replacing the diamond studs that are a traditional gift, Valeria wore gold filigreed earrings, that looked like the fringe on a traditional cowboy shirt. It was such a spectacle that even Valeria's priest cracked a smile at his charge's unique take on the hundreds-of-years-old tradition. The important part was, the tradition was still there. It wasn't just a physical transformation Valeria had undergone; in just a few weeks, she'd truly grown up.

The church ceremony ended at four. But since the Valeria at Twilight *quince* wouldn't start until ten p.m., Jamie, Carmen, and Alicia had devised a *quinceañera* scavenger hunt. Guests were divided into teams. Each team had to find fifteen iconic Austin items, ranging from a photo of the jaguar at the Austin zoo to a Lady Bird Johnson key chain from the presidential museum.

The scavenger hunt was designed to give the visitors a taste of the richness of Texas and locals a chance to see the state with new eyes. The bonus item, worth a full fifty out of a hundred points, was the autograph of one of Austin's most famous residents, actress Sandra Bullock, whom Gaz had passed more than a half a dozen times at the Starbucks closest to the South by Southwest headquarters.

For Amigas Inc., the scavenger hunt was a chance to put the finishing touches on the party. Just as they'd never done a makeover as radical as Valeria's, they'd never built a set as elaborate.

At ten, Valeria entered the great room, her dark eyes shining from beneath her sleek bangs. Omarion was at her side, handsome in his navy tuxedo jacket, white T-shirt, and dark blue jeans. Valeria, dressed in a short black minidress festooned with black feathers along the bodice and a pair of hot pink Converse sneakers, entered her party on a special ramp that Alicia had ordered (and then reordered in a smaller size so it could get through the front door). The ramp covered the Castillos' dramatic staircase. This was the big "reveal" that Alicia and her girls had been planning. As everyone watched, Valeria pulled a skateboard from behind her back and proceeded to skate down, looking as comfortable in her dress as she had at the skate park. The crowd let out whoops and hollers that only got louder when she held her skateboard over her head to show off its Yellow Rose of Texas design that Jamie had made.

Jamie and Carmen snapped multiple pictures with their phones—both for the Amigas Inc. portfolio and to send back home to Domingo and Dash. Jamie typed a quick message to her *novio* before she hit SEND: *See, Dash, another satisfied* quince. *Truly, I'm making a lot of people smile out here in Texas! Can you say the same about your golf game? J/K* ☺

Then Valeria changed into her Texas belle goth dress for the dancing portion of the night. It was a lacy black off-the-shoulder affair with a full skirt, and it made Valeria look like a modern-day Scarlett O'Hara. She gave a very princesslike twirl, and the guests whooped at the flash of hot pink in the crinoline hoopskirt.

For the live-music segment, Saniyah performed "Wheels of Texas" for Omarion and Valeria's dance. Then Gaz played a few of Valeria's favorite tunes, dedicating his last song to his "best girl, Alicia." He looked her straight in the eyes, full of a new confidence, and sang "Playing for Keeps," the song he had written especially for her. Then he pulled a huge surprise and announced that, with Saniyah's help, he'd signed a songwriting deal with Chia Pet, a small independent label based in Chicago.

Only the *amigas* noticed how Alicia gritted her teeth when Gaz mentioned Saniyah.

"Take it easy, tiger," Carmen whispered, stroking her friend's shoulder soothingly.

"He's with you, remember?" Jamie said reassuringly to her very best *amiga*. Alicia knew they were right and that she and Gaz were stronger than ever, but as much as she had learned and explored, and as much as she enjoyed Austin, there was a part of her that couldn't wait to be back home in Miami, with songwriting, singing, and dancing Saniyah hundreds of miles away.

Once the music switched to iPod tunes, the crowd slowed down to enjoy hors d'oeuvres featuring all of Valeria's favorite foods—cranberry and pecan tamales, roasted poblano peppers stuffed with sautéed corn and zucchini and topped with sour cream, chocolaty mole served over tofu (plus chicken, which was available for the nonvegetarians). But the real star of the evening was the sixty-four-foot-long chocolate buffet—featuring chocolate mousse, freshly made cakes, petit fours, homemade ice-cream sandwiches, cupcakes, chocolate-chip cookies, chocolate milk, chocolate bread pudding, chocolate fondue, and dozens of other sinfully delicious chocolate desserts.

Looking around at Valeria enjoying herself, the *tías* actually smiling, and the guests dancing, Alicia beamed. They had done it. Once again, they'd pulled off the sweetest of parties.

EPILOGUE

THE NEXT DAY, the Castillo family arranged a special good-bye for their guests and friends. As the sun set over the ranch, two pickup trucks drove up, ready to take everyone on a tour. The Amigas Inc. team and their new friends piled into the backs of the trucks, huddling under blankets and admiring one another's new looks. Everyone's outfit had a bit of Western flair, from Jamie's beautiful turquoise-colored vest to Carmen's long plaid skirt to Alicia's studded black leather cowboy boots.

As they rode deep into the property, they passed all kinds of animals they'd never seen live and in person before, from armadillos to Mexican tree frogs and big brown bats. Gaz and Saniyah played songs on their guitars. Alicia was happy to realize that Saniyah seemed to be entirely smitten with Omarion's best friend, Christian, with whom she had spent all night dancing at Valeria's *quince*. The others on the Amigas team were equally happy that Lici was leaving the singing to the professionals.

Valeria gave each of the Miami girls a special cowboy hat, explaining that in Texas there was a saying that some people were "All hat, no cattle." She wanted the Amigas group to know that their hats meant just the opposite—they were all hat, all cattle—meaning that they were the real deal.

Watching the sunset, Alicia, Carmen, Jamie, and Gaz all smiled. Texas had certainly left its mark: Gaz was no longer a member of Amigas Inc. Alicia had learned she couldn't control everything. And Jamie and Carmen had discovered new skills and friends. Valeria had said Texas would always have room for them, but more importantly, they would now have Texas in their hearts—always.

A Chat With Jennifer Lopez

When I first came up with the idea for the Amigas *series, I thought about the many Latina women who, like Alicia, Jamie, and Carmen, had started out as entrepreneurial teenagers. Who, through hard work, imagination, and dedication, were able to take their passions and talents and become role models and successful adults. For me, Jennifer Lopez is such a woman. She has incredible drive and an amazing work ethic, qualities she shares with the girls in* Amigas. *They, too, needed an equal amount of determination to turn their quince-party-planning business into a huge success.*

So, to get a better sense of this connection, I sat down with Jennifer, and we talked about quinces and what it was like for her as a Latina girl growing up in New York City. Here are some more of her answers....

—J. Startz

1. The Amigas are fortunate enough to have formed their own business, which provides them with summer and holiday employment. When you were a teenager, did you have any summer or part-time jobs? If so, what were they like? Were any of them memorable—because they were either (a) so great or (b) so bad?

My first summer job was sweeping up hair at a beauty salon. I was about twelve or thirteen years old. I really looked forward to going to work every day. Not because the job was so glamorous, but just because I always loved work. I loved getting my little ten dollars at the end of the week.

2. As a teenager, did you and your family or friends ever take car trips or vacations together? If so, what was the farthest you traveled away from home, and what kind of a trip was it?

Our first car trip was a vacation to Florida, to go to Disney World. We drove all the way from New York, which took two days! It felt like it took forever to get there. We drove in a station wagon, so my sisters and I would go lie down all the way in the back of the car sometimes. My mom loved listening to the radio, so we would sing a lot of songs and play games while we were on the road.

3. How did you get your start as a performer? Were you discovered, or, like Gaz, did you work on demos and try to shop them around to the industry? Did you have to deal with a lot of rejection? And, if so, what motivated you to keep at it?

I was like Gaz—I worked hard and tried to dance and

perform wherever I could! I knew from the beginning I didn't want to do only one thing—I wanted to sing and dance and act. So I worked on it all the time. I took classes and took small dance gigs in clubs or [for] music videos, until bigger jobs came along. This business is definitely one where you have to deal with rejection—even after you become successful. If you can keep going from there, that's what can separate you from someone who might not make it.

4. Saniyah, the Austin musician Gaz meets at South by Southwest, advises him that it is very crucial as a young artist to network with other people in the music industry. Do you see this as part of your job? Do you think this is an important skill for any professional to develop?

Yes, I think it's important to network, no matter what your profession is. When people know the person you are—that you are a good person—and they also know the talents that you have, that can give you an advantage.

5. Valeria's family are very proud of their Mexican heritage, and they all have a real love of authentic Tex-Mex foods. Your background is Puerto Rican. What are the traditional dishes from Puerto Rico that are your favorites? Does your family have any favorites?

I love all Puerto Rican food! I love pernil, arroz con gandules, platanos maduros. *My mom is the best cook—she makes a yummy* pastelón, *which is one of my favorites. But if she just makes white rice, red beans, and chicken cutlets, I'm still the happiest girl in the world.*

6. Gaz is torn between following his musical passion and helping with Amigas Inc. Were you like that or more like Alicia, who seems to know exactly what she wants?

I think I was more like Alicia. I always knew this was what I wanted to do. When I was about seventeen or eighteen, I had a dream one night that I was supposed to be an entertainer; I was supposed to be in this business. So, when I got old enough to choose between going to college and going out on my own to start working on my career, I chose working on my career.

7. Valeria's a unique character with an array of interests and hobbies. What about you?

The hobbies that I had were mostly sports: running track, softball, tennis. I loved to do things that were athletic. I still do!

8. By the end of the trip, both Alicia and Gaz feel really comfortable in Texas but at the same time excited to be going home. Have you ever found a place like that?

I felt that way in Miami. From the first time I went there, I felt like I was home. I think it was maybe because I didn't get to go to Puerto Rico much as a child . . . but Miami felt like it was part of me. It was partly because of its Latin culture, partly the tropical air; the sand and beaches. It wasn't until I went to Puerto Rico later on my own that I realized how similar they were—and that's why I felt connected to it. It was something innate in me; from my parents, from my heritage and upbringing. So I always felt like I belonged there, when I was in Miami. But, coming home is always the best, of course!

Make sure to RSVP for the next quinceañera!

Amigas
A Formal Affair

by Veronica Chambers

Created by Jane Startz
Inspired by Jennifer Lopez

CHAPTER 1

IT WAS A PERFECT October day in southern Miami. Cool and just breezy enough for the palm trees to sway, but still early enough in the season that the rains hadn't begun yet. Carmen Ramirez-Ruben walked down the hall of her school, Coral Gables High. At her left was her best friend in the entire world, Alicia Cruz, and at her right was her second bestie, Jamie Sosa.

One of the coolest things about living in Miami was the diversity of its people. This mix of peoples and cultures was truly reflected at C. G. High, where you really couldn't judge a book by its cover. There were Indian students who were of Arab descent and Pakistanis who were Hindu. Black students might be Latinos from the Dominican Republic and Panama, or African Americans, or Jamaicans or Saint Lucians. A blond, blue-eyed girl might be from Venezuela, and a dark-haired girl with olive skin might be from Kansas.

All this diversity didn't mean that there weren't cliques—the worst of which was the SoBees. They called themselves that because they planned all of the school's socials and benefits. Like the partners of Amigas Inc., the SoBees were a multicultural and multi-talented crew. But unlike the *amigas*—who, though well liked by their fellow students, were not interested in being part of the superpopular C.G. power elite—the SoBees were zealously dedicated to maintaining their elevated social status.

One member, Maya Clark-Hayward, was a tall, thin African American girl with café au lait skin and thick curly hair that looked like something out of a shampoo commercial. Her mother owned a string of radio stations nationwide, and the inside of Maya's locker was covered with photos of her and the singers and stars whom she had met when they stopped by the locally owned station to do promotions.

Another SoBee, April Yunayama, was Japanese American, and third-generation Miami elite. A collector of designer clothes, she was petite in stature and rail thin. April also loved to discuss people's looks and would ask her two BFF SoBees over and over, on a daily basis, whether the outfit she was wearing made her look fat.

And the third SoBee, Dorinda Carrassquillo, was a Dominican, who was notorious for being the most sarcastic person at C. G. High—and the unofficial head of the group. Her father owned several luxury-car dealerships all over the city. Though she only had a learner's permit, Dorinda had received a car—a Kelly green Escalade—for her *quinceañera*. And because she was too young to drive without an adult with a driver's license accompanying her, the family's maid, Jacinta, was forced to ride along with the SoBees everywhere they wanted to go.

As the three *amigas* neared their classroom, the SoBees were putting up posters for the winter formal. "*Hola, chicas*," Dorinda said, handing the *amigas* a snowflake-shaped Save the Date card. "This is going to be the best winter formal ever. You all will probably learn a thing or two for your little party-planning business."

At the words *little* and *party-planning*, Jamie lurched forward ever so slightly. Carmen put a calming hand on her shoulder and subtly shook her head. Now was not the time or place.

"Thanks," Alicia said, taking the card. Smiling, she began walking toward the classroom again, her friends close behind.

The SoBees were safely out of earshot when Jamie went ahead and let her Bronx show. "Amigas Inc. is *huge*. It's no 'little party-planning business.' Girls like her work my last nerve!"

"Forget about it," Alicia laughed. "They're just jealous. This is going to be our first school formal and I'm totally psyched. Even the SoBees can't ruin that for me."

"I agree," Carmen said. "And of course they're jealous. All they know how to do is spend their parents' money to make an event fabulous. They don't worry about budgets or making sure *other* people are happy." She cast a disapproving eye as the SoBees teetered away in their five-inch gladiator heels. "We have a *real* company. Our *quinces* are off the hook, and we make all our own loot."

The summer before, the three girls, joined by Alicia's then close friend—and now boyfriend—Gaspar (Gaz) Colón, had formed their own business, Amigas Incorporated. In what seemed like no time at all, they had become one of the most popular *quinceañera* (Sweet Fifteen) planners in the city—and beyond. Recently, Gaz had decided to quit the business to concentrate on his music, but he still provided playlists and performed at all of Amigas Incorporated's gigs. In an ironic twist, since leaving, Gaz's romance with Alicia had really bloomed; in large part it was because they no longer had to deal with the added tension of having to work together.

As Latinas, Alicia, Carmen, and Jamie knew first-hand just how important a *quince* was, not only to the girl who was turning fifteen, but to her entire family. Traditionally, a *quinceañera* marked a Latina's transition from child to woman, and the ceremony, which started at the church and often culminated in a huge party that lasted until the early hours of the morning, could be as big an event as a wedding. Some parents started saving for a girl's *quince* from the moment she was born. Amigas Inc. had planned *quinces* that ranged in budget from $1,000 to $25,000. It was pretty heady stuff for three girls who themselves had all just turned fifteen in the last year. But they had never backed down from a challenge. Ever! When they got together, there wasn't anything they couldn't do. Each girl brought with her to the business a rich cultural heritage and a unique talent.

While the three *amigas* had worked hard over the last year, that didn't mean they hadn't played hard, too. Every chance they got, they took off for the beach, hung out at Alicia's house, or checked out one of their favorite hotel pools.

And then there was the dating. That had to be fit in between school, the job, and friend time. But they made it work. Alicia and Gaz were going strong and were the longest lasting couple of the group.

Even the impossible-to-please Jamie was hooked up with someone. Amigas Inc.'s resident artist had grown up in the South Bronx, or the boogie-down, as she liked to call it. A dark-skinned Latina whose family came from the Dominican Republic, she had a blunt and sometimes brutal take on things, which she called "keeping it real." Amazing though it seemed, Jamie was still dating Dash Mortimer, the salsa-dancing, Spanish-speaking, top-ranked teen golf star she had met when Amigas Inc. had been hired to plan a *quince* for his sister, Bianca. Although Jamie was loath to admit it, it had pretty much been love at first sight for both of them, and they had been nearly inseparable ever since.

And then there were Carmen and Domingo. The gorgeous computer nerd–über hottie and Carmen were practically attached at the hip. Domingo had become a fixture at her house; the couple spent hours together, and when they couldn't see each other, Domingo would send Carmen little love texts to let her know he was thinking about her. It seemed picture perfect.

But at that moment, standing in the hall, when

Carmen knew she should have been smiling and laughing and planning for the big dance, she wasn't. Her smile seemed frozen, forced.

Because she and Domingo were over. And she had no date for the dance. And even though she would never have dared admit it out loud, thinking about Domingo still hurt . . . a lot.

CHAPTER 2

IT HAD BEEN two months now, but Carmen still couldn't believe that she and Domingo were done. And the worst part was, she had been the one to initiate it.

Domingo had been a *chambelán*—sort of like a knight, without the shining armor—at Carmen's *quinceañera*, a Lati-Jew-na affair that Amigas Inc. had planned to reflect all the different elements of her background. Domingo had also been the first boy that she'd kissed, the first boy that she'd ever taken home to meet her parents, and the first boy who had motivated her parents to call out, "Leave the door open," whenever the couple went upstairs to her room.

Then Domingo had gotten into his dream school: Savannah College of Art and Design. In Georgia. A full 485 miles away. He planned to study interactive media and video-game design. Although he hadn't chosen it because of her, it was also a school with an excellent program in fashion, and Carmen was a gifted designer. She sewed all of her own clothes, and everything she wore looked as though it had come straight from some major couture house. If in two years, when Carmen was ready for college, they were still together, it might be nice if they were to go to the same school. That was what they told each other: *It might be nice.* No pressure. No heavy-duty plans. Just an open door that beckoned with possibility.

At the beginning of the summer, before Domingo left for college, they had sat side by side on Carmen's bed, cell phones in hand, open to their calendars. They had mapped out trips that would lessen the amount of time they'd be separated from one another. He would come back to Miami for a weekend at the end of September, so they'd never spend more than twenty-one days apart. Carmen's mother, under the impression that they'd be starting college visits early, had agreed to take Carmen to Savannah for a weekend in late October or early November. Domingo would be back for Thanksgiving, and after that it was a short sixteen-day sprint until he was home for Christmas break. It was going to be so simple, really. They'd concentrate on work when they were apart. They would focus only on each other when they were together. And thank God for Skype and free rollover cell-phone minutes. They would make it. They had to. . . . Things were so good between them.

Together, they could spend hours, working side by side, speaking in a kind of abbreviated sign language. Domingo would tap away at his computer. Carmen would jump from her sketchbook to her sewing machine. Every once in a while, they stopped to show each other something. One or the other would nod, offer a suggestion, walk over, and plant a kiss on their beloved's lips. But mostly, there was this beautiful silence. The hum of two people who needed few words to communicate what was in their hearts.

Which was why, a few weeks before Domingo was scheduled to head to Georgia, Carmen started to have a sickening feeling in the pit of her stomach. She'd begun to feel that, as much as she loved Domingo, they were Alicia and Gaz in reverse. Alicia and Gaz had first spent years as best friends, with a frisson of tension underneath the surface, but never enough to spark anything real—until finally, they got it together and started dating. Carmen feared that she and Domingo were the exact opposite: all sparks at the start, but, with the increased distance between them, bound to fall into the just-friends category, until there was nothing but the memory of romance.

Because she'd sensed it, because she'd spent so many quiet hours with Domingo, she wasn't surprised when he rang the doorbell unexpectedly one hot August afternoon. It was as though she had willed him to come over. And the look on his face didn't surprise her, either. It mirrored her own—a desire to be together forever, mingled with the realization that they needed to break up.

"Go on a boat ride with me?" Domingo asked. He handed her a hastily wrapped bouquet of wildflowers that looked as though he might have picked them himself. They were her favorite kind.

"Of course," she answered as she took the flowers into the kitchen and looked for just the right unfussy vase to put them in. Settling on a butter yellow ceramic pitcher, she put the flowers into water and grabbed her keys as she walked out the door.

In the boat, Domingo rowed, as he usually did. She liked to watch him, marveling at how his light brown arms moved with such graceful precision. On especially hot days, like this one, she could see his sunglasses begin to steam up. She wanted to be patient, to let him be the one to raise the topic of separating, of them each beginning school with a completely fresh start. But she couldn't help herself. In the Ramirez-Ruben household, you spoke early if you wanted to be heard.

"I don't want to break up, but I think we should break up," she whispered, staring down at the bottom of the boat.

"But I don't want to date other people," Domingo mumbled, looking away from her.

"Me, neither," Carmen added. "But I don't think this is about other people. I want this to end when we're still happy with one another. Instead of waiting until you feel like it is a burden to come see me, or that it takes you away from the life you should be leading with all your heart and soul, almost five hundred miles away."

"*Mi amor*, let's not say the words," Domingo implored her. "Let's not use the words *break up* or *ending* or *done* or *finished*. Not now. Not yet."

Carmen leaned across the little turquoise rowboat and put both of her hands on his. "Is *I will always love you* okay?"

Domingo nodded and kissed her.

Carmen pulled away and looked at him now, not afraid anymore, not wanting to look anywhere else.

"Is *I'll miss you* okay?" she asked.

"I think it is," Domingo replied. But this time when he kissed her, she could feel his tears wet her cheek, taste them salty against his skin.

Then he did something unexpected. He laughed. "We're too mature," Domingo said, quickly wiping the tears from his face. "I mean, look at us. We're sitting here being all cool. Why aren't you screaming?"

"I know what you mean," she agreed. "We should drag this out. Have a big nasty fight around Thanksgiving . . ."

"We could make up around December twelfth, after I take my last final," Domingo continued, playfully.

Carmen laughed then, too. "But the thing to do would be to totally ruin Christmas. We'd have to break up again. And out of decency, we'd both have to spend the entire Christmas and New Year's in mourning. Which would suck."

Domingo began to row the little boat back to the Ramirez-Ruben family dock. "If we break up now," he wondered aloud, "would I be over you by Christmas?"

Carmen raised an eyebrow. "Possibly. But remember, we weren't going to use the words *break up*."

"So what do you suggest?" Domingo asked, as he tied the rowboat to the little dock and helped Carmen onto the shore.

Carmen smiled, held his hand, then kissed him with all the wild abandon of a *telenovela* star. "We've got six days before you leave for college. Let's see how many different ways we can come up with to say, 'I love you.'"

Domingo placed his hands over his heart, then pointed at Carmen and smiled.

"What's that?" Carmen asked curiously.

"It's sign language for *I love you*," Domingo replied, slinging an arm around Carmen's shoulder as they walked back into the Ramirez-Ruben home. "There's a busboy at Bongos who's hearing-impaired. He's been teaching a bunch of us at the restaurant how to sign."

"Let me see that again," Carmen asked coyly, as they stood at her front door.

Domingo repeated the gesture.

Carmen shook her head. "I don't think that means *I love you*."

"Really?" Domingo asked, his eyes widening. "I didn't know you signed. What does it mean?"

"It means *please don't put so much starch in my shirt*" Carmen said, before collapsing in giggles.

Domingo smiled. "Very funny, *loca*. How will I ever find anyone who makes me laugh the way you do?"

To be continued . . .